CW01431436

ALEX WAGNER

THE WEDNESDAY EVENING EVENING CLUB

A Case for the Master Sleuths

1

The journey had begun with a promise from our human that sounded most enticing to a sled dog like me.

"It will be so much cooler in the South Tyrolean Alps than here at our lake, Athos," Victoria had announced to me with a beaming smile. "You and Pearl will feel right at home there."

As a descendant of the proud wolves of Alaska, I am equipped with fur that is able to defy the iciest winter storms. In the summer heat, however, it is far less suitable. Pearl, my favorite cat and sometimes the worst nuisance, is also well wrapped, but usually lies around so lazily that the heat does not bother her so much.

High summer had already arrived at our lake at the beginning of June, and so I was impatiently awaiting the promised cooling holiday in the mountains. I had heard of South Tyrol before, even if I could no longer remember where or from whom. It is supposedly in Italy, which is strange, since Tyrol in general and East Tyrol in particular belong to Austria. North or West Tyrol apparently do not exist; at least I had never heard of them. In South Tyrol lots of people seem to speak German, despite the region's Italian situation. The humans are sometimes really not very logical. But no matter.

The area looked gorgeous, even as we arrived; we were surrounded on all sides by high mountain peaks covered in dense forests. But Victoria was clinging to the steering wheel of her car, struggling up a narrow winding road at a snail's pace, and looking so green in the face that it seemed she might throw up at any moment. I guess high mountains and tight curves weren't her thing. She smelled terribly anxious, so I would have liked to run my tongue over her ear to comfort her.

But then again, maybe that wasn't such a good idea: first of all, she didn't appreciate such caresses, and second, I would no doubt have ended up distracting her, and we could all—Victoria, Pearl and me—have ended up in the gorge that gaped open beside us like the mouth of a hungry dragon.

The alpine peaks were jagged and devoid of vegetation; some of them were even covered with snow. Victoria pointed out this impressive panorama to Pearl and me, but she herself did not dare to take her eyes off the road for more than half a second.

And as for the promised cooling: not only was the engine of Victoria's car already nearly boiling, but the air conditioning was also struggling against the enormous summer heat that we had apparently brought with us from Austria. The car was puffing and groaning, almost as if it were not a machine but a living being—one that desperately needed a break.

Victoria's forehead was dripping with sweat, which she didn't seem at all happy about, but I envied her for it. We dogs do not have this gift; we can only sweat from our paws, and just to a very limited extent. The only halfway effective way to cool ourselves down is to pant—which I was doing extensively, still hardly able to alleviate the sauna-like feeling in the car.

Pearl lay languidly next to me on the back seat, and I couldn't tell if she was just taking a nap or also suffering from nausea and therefore shutting up for once. I wondered if the heat was tormenting her as much as it was me. Since we'd reached the foot of the mountain, whose flank we were now fighting our way up along, she had not made any sound, and I had already learned to leave her alone when she was taciturn. Cats are known to be very capricious creatures.

The reason we were traveling here to Italy, and were now struggling up a South Tyrolean Alpine road, was Diana Leonhardt. She had called Victoria a few days ago and asked for her help. From what I'd been able to pick up from the conversation, Diana had been Victoria's client a long time ago—in her younger years, as she put it—and had apparently become a friend in the process.

Our human is what the two-leggeds call a psychotherapist. She repairs sick souls, usually doing nothing but talking to the other suffering two-leggeds. Lately, however, she had all but given up the job and was in the process of reorienting herself professionally, as she put it. This phase had been going on for several months now, but for Diana Leonhardt Victoria was apparently willing to make an exception.

What kind of psychological support Diana needed, I hadn't really managed to overhear during the phone call. In any case, she seemed to be in very bad mental shape, suffering great anxiety, and she had therefore begged Victoria to join her in South Tyrol and spend a few weeks of luxury vacation in her family castle.

Family castle—that sounded very tempting to me as a historically-minded four-legged. I also associated the word *luxury* with juicy steaks, rooms with wonderfully cool marble floors, and maybe even a swimming pool where I could splash around a bit.

Pearl was just as excited about the new client—and the trip south—although for different reasons.

"It's a good thing Victoria wants to investigate what's got this poor woman so scared," she'd told me after the phone call had ended. "This is exactly the kind of training she needs to become a capable assistant for us."

Pearl had of course listened attentively to the telephone conversation, just like me. I guess you could say that the midget and I are two morbidly curious pets. As for what she meant by *assistant,* that was the latest crazy idea that she'd gotten into her head: Pearl wanted to turn our human into a capable sleuth to help us with our investigations.

You see, dear reader, Pearl and I are detectives; the best in the world, according to the tiny one. Pearl is not one for the old adage that modesty is a virtue. She may not be of an impressive size, but her personality is that of a royal tigress.

Pearl and I had been involved in murder cases—among the two-leggeds—already twice before in the last few months, and both times we had been able to

8

hunt down the killer in the end. However we'd had to struggle with certain hurdles. For example, we could not question witnesses in the way that human investigators are able to, because two-leggeds are known to be incapable of understanding our language. For the same reason we couldn't share our knowledge, our investigative findings, with the humans either, which is equally annoying. Therefore, Pearl had come to the conclusion that we needed a human assistant, and this person should be Victoria.

I didn't really know what to make of her idea. Of course Pearl's arguments made sense to me; the pipsqueak might be conceited and sometimes altogether too cocky when it came to assessing danger, but she certainly wasn't stupid.

On the other hand we pets are also responsible for the safety of our humans, and the idea of putting Victoria in danger through our detective activities did not appeal to me at all.

Only recently we had come to the conclusion—in this instance Pearl and I had even agreed—that Victoria needed a new man in her life, and we had succeeded in our mission perfectly. Victoria and Tim, our neighbors' former gardener, were now a couple fiercely in love and already busy making plans for a future together.

However, Tim had not been able to go with us to South Tyrol; he had enrolled over the summer in a so-called entrepreneurship course, which was taking place in Vienna. He wanted to learn everything he needed to know in order to set up his own gardening business. As an assistant detective he was therefore out of the running.

As I mentioned earlier, Victoria, on the other hand, was actively searching for a new vocation, as psychotherapy no longer filled her with joy. So maybe she would quite happily become a sleuth if we nudged her in the right direction?

"Listen, Pearl," I'd said to the little cat, while Victoria was already beginning her preparations for the trip to South Tyrol. "This Diana Leonhardt may suffer anxiety, but that doesn't mean she's in any real danger, or even that someone is trying to take her life. So maybe this time there's nothing to investigate at all—and certainly no case to train our assistant detective on, as you have envisaged. Victoria's clients often just imagine their problems, you know. And murders really don't happen every day; people aren't that violent. It was a huge coincidence that we've already been involved in two murders in such a short time."

"Wait and see," Pearl only said, obstinate as ever. Solving murder cases really was her new obsession. She also spent a lot of time educating herself in her new role—when she wasn't eating some delicacy or devoting herself to grooming her fluffy white fur.

Neither Pearl nor I were able to read human books, so we only had TV to further our education. Victoria, however, preferred to have her nose stuck in books rather than spending many hours in front of the television.

But Pearl was not discouraged by this hurdle. With the patience of an angel—and the weapons of the cutest kitten, which no one can resist—she trained Victoria to become a crime and thriller fan, at least as far as the evening program was concerned.

If Victoria made herself comfortable in front of the TV, instead of reaching for a book, there was a reward in the form of cuddles from the tiny one ... but only if Victoria tuned in to the *right* TV program. In other words, if she watched a detective story, or at least a program in which two-leggeds were murdered and then someone had to find out how and why, and above all who was responsible for the bloody deed.

When Victoria had an inkling to watch a romance or historical movie, Pearl would jump off her lap snarling like a tiger and then sulk for a few hours. Historical films or even documentaries would have been quite to *my* taste, but of course, as so often was the case, I was not asked.

What can I say—the training program worked. Fortunately Victoria had always been a quick learner. For a few weeks now almost nothing but mystery shows had been on our evening viewing schedule, and Victoria actually seemed to enjoy detective stories and detective work, at least on television. And if she didn't feel like watching a movie herself or went out in the evening, she kept the TV set—and the appropriate program—on for Pearl. Cats really are a bit crazy, don't you think? And sometimes they're quite scary.

But back to our journey to South Tyrol: as we were

huffing, puffing and sweating our way up the serpentine roads to Diana Leonhardt's castle, I fervently hoped that a peaceful vacation lay ahead of us and not a murder case in which we could further our quest to train Victoria to be an assistant detective. I am not as bloodthirsty as Pearl; I wasn't longing to be chasing a killer again. But I was hopeful, as I said, that the likelihood of such a crime was vanishingly small.

I had no idea...

2

When we finally reached the castle, the sun was already setting. I could breathe a little easier as the intense heat relented somewhat.

Victoria, Pearl and I climbed out of the car in front of a building that was truly impressive. Victoria's father, who had been a professor of history as well as my former human, would have loved it.

"Very eclectic mix of styles," he'd liked to say when he'd set eyes on such a property, the type that seemed to have grown organically over the centuries.

In my humble—and not really expert—opinion, the thing was less a castle and more of a fully-fledged fortress. It was perched on a kind of cliff, at the end of a private road that branched off from the steep winding motorway we had crawled up earlier. Where the parking lot lay, and also to the left and to the right, the building was surrounded by a thoroughly shaded park, as I happily discovered, and the castle itself had thick walls with fortified corner towers and battlements.

Thick walls, that means cool rooms, I said to myself delightedly—but perhaps, in view of the nightmare that was to await us here, I must not conceal the fact that a chill ran down my spine at the mere sight of the old structure.

The most unusual thing about the building was its color: it was not gray, or sand-colored like so many other old castles, but a deeply somber black.

You might have thought we'd lost our way and arrived in Transylvania, at the castle of Count Dracula—a character I knew from television, and I still don't know whether he'd actually lived or had merely sprung from the imagination of the two-leggeds. In any case, this count did not seem to be a particularly nice fellow, and I would not have felt any desire to spend my summer vacation in his castle, no matter how pleasantly cool his rooms might be.

But back to the castle that actually lay before us: although the last rays of sunlight were still illuminating the building, and it was definitely not in the possession of a vampire lord, it seemed gloomy, almost eerie to me. But I am really not a fearful dog—not that I'm giving you that impression right now!

Numerous oriels and decorations on the facade softened the severity of the building somewhat, but bright red vines clinging to the walls around the main gate made the whole thing look even creepier. At first glance one might have thought that blood was oozing from the black facade...

Who in their right mind would build such a house?

I also noticed that the estate as a whole was huge. And only *one* family was supposed to be living here? The Leonhardts were clearly not only quite strange, but also very wealthy—which was perhaps the cause of Diana's psychological distress.

Naturally I cannot call myself an expert in matters of the soul like Victoria, but as far as the humans' money goes, it's usually like this in my opinion: the greater the wealth, the worse the mental pain of the two-leggeds in question often is.

We were first welcomed on the forecourt of the castle by a very friendly maid, but right behind her appeared the castle dragon. It was not a literal scaly reptile, but an elderly woman who actually looked very pretty, smelled of violets and roses, and wore an equally flower-bedecked dress. But it was her nature that seemed to me to be that of a dragon, who liked to eat dogs, cats and even other two-leggeds for breakfast.

The woman received us with a disparaging look and a cool greeting that barely crossed her lips.

She introduced herself as Barbara Messner, 'the sister of the late master of the house.' "And you must be the psychologist," she said to Victoria. "Dr. Adler. We've been expecting you."

Those were her words, not rude on the surface; but the way she pronounced *psychologist* and Victoria's doctoral degree, and especially the way she eyed our human from head to toe while doing so, she probably could have honestly been saying, "*People like you are not welcome here. Unless they want to end up in the cooking pot.*"

Well, I will admit that perhaps my imagination was running away with me for a bit there, but can I truly be blamed for it, considering the creepy castle and this scary old woman?

I myself earned a somewhat more benevolent if penetrating look from Barbara Messner.

In a tone of voice that seemed to immediately drop the temperature around us by ten degrees, she said to Victoria, "Handsome dog you have there, but he really doesn't belong in our temperate zone."

With a sideways glance at Pearl, she added, "And I guess your kitten is still very young, isn't it? Or is it one of those newfangled dwarf breeds? Don't you think it's irresponsible to take her on such a long journey?"

Victoria put on her friendliest therapist's face. I could smell that Barbara was stressing her out with her gruff manner, but she didn't let it show.

"Pearl is already a fully-grown cat," she explained to the dragon, "she has only remained a kitten on the outside because of, um, a genetic peculiarity. And she loves to travel."

Genetic peculiarity.

Most people said *genetic defect* or *genetic mutation*. But for Victoria—and in my eyes as well—Pearl had no defect. Apart from her sometimes overly-dominant personality, perhaps. And she wasn't a mutant, either; that sounded kind of like a horror movie, we'd all agreed.

Barbara Messner wrinkled her nose. "A hereditary defect, you mean to say? How awful. The poor thing! Wouldn't it be more humane to have her put down? So many of these tortured souls kept alive at all costs these days! Even among us humans. Wouldn't it be much better to let them go home to the Lord and spare them all this suffering?"

Victoria took a deep breath. Her hands had clenched into fists, and it must have taken her some effort to open them again—instead of going for the old woman's throat.

"I assure you," she said in a polite, but now rather icy tone, "Pearl may be small on the outside, but she is most definitely not limited in any way. She has the personality of an adult tigress."

My thoughts exactly. Perhaps Victoria was slowly learning to understand our language after all, or even to read our thoughts?

"And she's certainly not suffering," she added emphatically.

"Yes, of course," Barbara said quickly. "After all, it's none of my business. Forgive me. Diana and her episodes have thrown me a little—well—off track. A woman shouldn't let herself go like that, especially not in front of her underage child." She clicked her tongue disapprovingly.

The sun had by now disappeared completely behind the castle, and its black walls rose menacingly into the sky. Clouds were clustering above our heads, appearing as if from nowhere. A stiff breeze, which had arisen just as suddenly, made the blood-red vine leaves rustle as if they wanted to whisper a warning to us. *Abandon all hope, ye who enter here....*

Where had I heard those words before? Probably somewhere on television. Maybe I should get Pearl to watch fewer gory shows in the future.

At least Victoria's promise seemed to have come true

now. I was actually not feeling blazing hot anymore, now that we had arrived in South Tyrol. Quite the opposite....

"*Let herself go?*" Victoria repeated in alarm, staring into the dragon woman's eyes. "What happened? Is Diana all right?"

Again Barbara wrinkled her nose. "Well, you're the psychotherapist, aren't you? If you ask me, Diana's not quite right in the head—she's completely lost it. Or she's just been boozing too much, if I may be so blunt."

She shook her head disapprovingly, then with a stiff gesture invited us to come inside.

"I'll show you to your room, Dr. Adler; everything is already prepared. After that you can check on your patient right away. She needs you urgently, it seems to me."

3

Our lodgings comprised three rooms that looked just like a museum. The colors were quite subdued, to match the exterior of the castle, but the furnishings were beautiful and the space was so large that Pearl and I simply had to play a game of tag right away.

As we did so, rushing through the entire suite and taking possession of it, and sniffing everything, I pretended as always—for Pearl's sake—that I couldn't catch up with her because she was such a fast runner. Granted, she is indeed quite a speedster considering how short her legs are, and as a Malamute I am a pack dog, after all, and not a sprinter.

There was a bedroom with a huge double bed, a living room with an equally generous seating area, and in addition a third room that seemed like a mixture of library, drawing room and study. It contained an open fireplace, many well-filled bookshelves, and a large desk. The woods were all shades from dark brown to black, the sofa was upholstered in blood-red velvet, and over the bed hung a heavy black canopy with cords of the same color. Count Dracula would have been delighted.

The furniture seemed very old to me, even though it looked brand new at the same time. Perhaps the pieces had been purchased for a lot of money and then lovingly restored by a real professional expert. They smelled of centuries-old woods and beeswax polish, and they shone so beautifully that one would have loved to chew on their legs. But of course, being the good dog that I am, I managed to restrain myself.

The bathroom had a large corner tub and an extra shower, and both the floor and walls were tiled with marble. I love marble—not because I am a snob like Pearl, but because the stone makes a wonderfully cool surface to lie on. It's a bit hard, but you can't have it all, can you?

Barbara Messner's reception might have been icy, but judging by this guest accommodation Victoria was more than welcome at the castle.

She quickly changed, then put a bowl of water and two food bowls on the floor for Pearl and me. She had packed only dry food for the trip—which I could understand, although Pearl turned up her nose in displeasure. The midget was a real gourmet and preferred to eat fresh fish, but that would have been all but impossible to transport, especially since it was thirty-five degrees Celsius in the shade outside.

Victoria gave us a few minutes to fortify ourselves, and then we made our way to Diana's bedroom, where Barbara had directed us. It was just getting dark outside, but Diana apparently liked to go to bed early. According to Barbara's unfriendly hints, she was a layabout who got up late in the morning and retired to her bedroom early at night ... usually armed with a bottle of wine.

The room in question was situated just two doors down from our guest paradise on the first floor of the castle, so we didn't have to wander around the huge manor to find it.

Victoria knocked timidly on the door, which was immediately opened by a slim, dark-haired man—a smoker, as my nose didn't fail to notice. He didn't seem to know who Victoria was at first, just looking at her in confusion instead of inviting her into the room.

Pearl took the initiative. She dashed between the humans' legs, which I couldn't have done without bringing both the man and Victoria down. But at least I could see that the tiny one was running towards the large bed that dominated the room. In it, supported by a veritable mountain of pillows, sat a woman with tangled reddish-blond hair, pale cheeks and eyes that were staring at us with pure fear.

Diana Leonhardt, I guessed. I estimated her to be in her early forties, and she would certainly have been a very beautiful woman if she hadn't looked so worn.

But when she caught sight of Pearl—who had promptly jumped onto the bed—the terror in her eyes abruptly gave way to an expression of delight. She let out a little cry—a sound of excitement, not of fright—and then stretched out her hands to Pearl. "Oh, God, you're cute! Hello, you sweet little kitty!"

This kind of reaction was already well known to me; I'd observed it many times in a practically identical form. The humans, whether big or small, sick or healthy, fearful or in the best of moods ... they all loved the midget. Pearl knew this, of course, and shamelessly exploited her effect on the two-leggeds, usually for her own purposes. Now, however, she seemed merely curious about our new client.

A second man, looking very much like the first but who had been sitting on the edge of Diana's bed, now rose and approached Victoria with a friendly smile. He had striking green eyes, a very strong jawline and seemed to know immediately who Victoria was. He greeted her by name and politely asked her to come in.

He introduced himself and the other man: "I am Sendrik Leonhardt, Diana's husband, and this is Bastian, my brother. We're so glad you could make arrangements to join us, Dr. Adler. And with such delightful company to boot." His gaze wandered from me to Pearl, who had taken possession of Diana's lap and was letting herself be cuddled while purring comfortably.

Victoria shook hands with both men, asked that they simply call her Victoria instead of the more formal *Dr. Adler,* and then walked briskly toward Diana—who joyfully held out her arms.

"Vicky! You look fantastic, not a day older than I remember. Come give me a hug! I'm so glad you're here."

At her last words, some of the fear I'd previously registered in Diana's eyes returned.

And something else struck me: Diana was giving off a distinct odor of alcohol. I guessed vodka, but she had also drunk a large amount of wine before that—or at the same time?

The older I get, the better I have learned to distinguish the smell of the many different alcoholic beverages that the two-leggeds love so much. Even though they all burn in my nose, they each give off a very different stench. In my opinion, it is wine that still smells the best.

When Victoria had sat down at Diana's bedside, Pearl jumped back onto the floor, and the two women hugged like old friends.

Sendrik and Bastian stood a few steps away, and I noticed that Diana's husband was measuring his brother with a suspicious look—which the latter didn't seem to notice. Bastian's eyes were fixed intently on the two women.

"Diana is about to fall asleep," Sendrik told Victoria. "I injected her with a strong sedative just before you came."

He pointed to a small glass vial with a tightly written, pale yellow label that was sitting on the nightstand, and which was only half full. Next to it lay a used syringe.

Victoria raised her eyebrows in amazement at the sight.

"Sendrik is a doctor, you see," Diana explained, "a plastic surgeon, actually—well respected, with a popular practice in Bolzano. But he also takes such wonderful care of me, don't you, darling? And right now he's on vacation and can be with us all day ... with me and Juno. That's my daughter from my first marriage, remember her? She's nearly sixteen now, but very sickly, I'm afraid; she has a terribly delicate constitution—"

Diana gasped for air. She had been speaking faster and faster, not taking a single breath between her explanations.

Sendrik hurried toward the bed and settled on the other edge of it, opposite Victoria.

"Honey, calm down," he said gently, at the same time taking Diana's hand. "You need to rest for now, okay? Victoria will be staying with us for quite a while, after all, won't you?" he said, addressing our human.

Victoria nodded. "Of course."

She patted Diana's other hand and spoke soothingly to her. "Get some sleep now, and we'll talk tomorrow morning, okay?"

The two might not have seen each other for a long time, but you could tell they were still good friends.

Our human looked lovingly concerned, while Diana had a relieved expression now that she knew Victoria would stand by her.

"It's fine," she said, "and thank you for coming, Vicky!" She smiled wanly, and the next moment her eyelids were already beginning to flicker. The sedative Sendrik had mentioned seemed to be taking effect.

The doctor lifted his wife's hand, which was growing increasingly limp, to his lips and kissed it gently. Then he rose from the edge of the bed.

"Come on, Victoria," he said, "let's give her a chance to rest."

4

Bastian hesitated, but then he left the room, together with the other two.

Pearl and I followed the humans. Sendrik gently closed the door behind us, and Victoria began bombarding him with questions. "What happened? Ms. Messner welcomed us, but then she suggested that Diana had suffered some kind of seizure?"

Sendrik laughed bitterly. "Barbara, that old harpy. What did she tell you? That my wife is not right in the head—that she's become a drunkard?"

Victoria had the grace to look embarrassed. "That's just about how it sounded, I must confess. Of course I didn't believe her. I don't allow myself to be influenced by third-party opinions when it comes to my diagnosis of one of my clients. But please tell me what really happened. Why did you have to give Diana a sedative?"

"Those damned ghost stories freak her out," Bastian exclaimed. "The Wednesday Evening Club! She always sees ghosts for days afterwards, has nightmares—and she tries to suppress them with alcohol, I'm afraid. But she doesn't want to miss a single damn session no matter the cost!"

Sendrik gave his brother a slightly hostile look. Then he turned to our human again, speaking in a much more controlled tone than Bastian had: "I'm not a psychologist like you, Victoria, but it seems to me that Diana is increasingly suffering from delusions. This has been going on for several weeks now, and—"

He paused and walked a few steps down the corridor, away from Diana's room. He probably wanted to be completely sure that she would not overhear the conversation, even if she probably had long since sunk into a deep sleep.

Victoria and Bastian hurried after him, while Pearl and I stayed where we had settled. We didn't want to look like we were too interested in the two-leggeds' conversation. That kind of thing didn't go over well—after all, the humans didn't know that we could understand their language, or even that we were particularly interested in their affairs. Both Pearl and I had excellent hearing; a few meters' distance was no problem at all, especially since the two-leggeds were speaking in a very excited tone.

"Delusions, you say?" Victoria picked up the conversation again. "Of what sort? What specifically happened today?"

Sendrik's face contorted into a pained expression. "Diana hears and sees things that aren't really there. Today, for example, she retired early after dinner, because she was suffering from a headache. And then she suddenly thought she heard a wolf howl, presumably just as she dozed off. More precisely, the death rattle of a werewolf—those were her exact words. She was beside herself with fear."

He glanced at his brother, then directed a question at him: "Were you with her when she claimed to have heard the rattle?"

Did I hear a hint of reproach in Sendrik's voice? He and his brother didn't seem to me to be the best of friends, even though they looked very much alike. Both were powerfully built, and—to human eyes certainly—handsome men with dark hair, even if Bastian was probably a few years younger, or at least he had retained his youthful appearance. I estimated him to be perhaps forty-five, while Sendrik had definitely already passed fifty. On the other hand, the older man smelled much better—he was a non-smoker who wore a spicy male scent, while Bastian seemed to me to be surrounded by an eternal cloud of nicotine.

In response to Sendrik's question, Bastian shook his head. "No. I ... I happened to be coming down the stairs by chance when I heard Diana scream. That's why I rushed into her room. She hadn't locked the door, fortunately. I got there a minute before you, tops. I didn't see or hear anything, and certainly not a werewolf!"

"*By chance*, huh?" said Sendrik, giving his brother a hostile look.

Then he sighed softly, shrugged, and turned back to Victoria. "I didn't hear anything either. Well, except for Diana's scream."

He pointed with his thumb to a door just a few feet away from Diana's room.

"My bedroom is right next door," he explained. "We sleep separately ... because Diana wants it that way. Supposedly I snore terribly and toss and turn in bed at night, waking her up all the time," he added with a disarming smile, which transformed him into a shy youngster for a moment. "Even further to the left are our private quarters, a living room, my home office, and our music room—I just had the TV on, so I didn't really notice Diana's scream at first. Only when it got louder..."

Bastian took a step toward his brother, tapping his chest accusingly with his index finger. "Diana drinks too much; that's why she's having these damn hallucinations. Can't you see that? You can't just stand by and watch her booze herself into a full-on delirium!"

Now Sendrik's calm was gone. "That's so typical of you!" he burst out. "Of course it's my fault again! You think I don't try to keep Diana from drinking? But I'm her husband, not her jailer!—I can't *make* her do anything, and I can't just forbid her to drink!"

Bastian snorted like an angry bull, but said nothing in reply.

"Please calm down," Victoria told the two men. "So you think Diana sees—or hears—these things when she's drunk? Alcohol-induced delusions?"

"At least that's how it looks to me," Sendrik confirmed dejectedly. "But please, make up your own mind. I'm really very glad you were able to arrange your visit with us. Diana won't talk to me about her problems; to be frank I think she's ashamed in a way."

"That is sadly rather common among my clients," Victoria said. "Mental health problems or even full-blown illnesses are still a taboo subject in our society, unfortunately. People tend to sweep them under the rug, as if the sufferer were a leper."

Bastian snorted again and muttered something that sounded like "Diana is definitely not a nutcase."

"I think you'll find, Victoria," Sendrik said, taking the floor again and ignoring his brother, "that our house is full of eerie artifacts. The exterior facade says it all, doesn't it? Added to that, here inside the castle there are morbid paintings and sculptures, dark ancestral portraits like something out of a horror movie, display cases full of gruesome collectibles, and a color scheme like something out of a Victorian Gothic novel. Diana, however, won't get rid of it at any price. Neither will Juno, my stepdaughter. Both love spooky stories and try to preserve the memory of Diana's deceased first husband, Alexander Messner—Juno's father. His family had this castle built over a hundred and fifty years ago, and the Messners have always had a penchant for all things melancholic. For ghost and spook stories, for monsters, vampires, shapeshifters, and witches.... I think they seriously believe in these phenomena, these backwoods hicks. And who knows, maybe some of them even sucked on the necks of young ladies on dark nights—"

"I'm sorry," he interrupted himself, "I don't want to speak ill of the dead. However, the Messners have set up their castle as a sort of mausoleum, a fortress of madness, if you ask me, which certainly can't be conducive to the tranquility of an unstable person's psyche. And that's what Diana is, right? Unstable, I mean. She has after all been under your care before—for anxiety, as she mentioned to me once."

Victoria nodded, but she did not reveal any details of the treatment she had provided at that time. She always maintained strict confidentiality regarding her clients; only with Pearl and me did she occasionally talk about one or other particularly difficult case.

We didn't know anything about Diana, though; she'd been undergoing treatment with Victoria before the midget or I had even been born.

But I had learned in the meantime that the souls of some two-leggeds are incurable. They often spend their whole lives fighting against fears, compulsions, and delusions, even if a therapist like Victoria devotedly takes care of them. Sometimes you really do feel sorry for the poor humans.

Sendrik continued: "The Messners also started the Wednesday Evening Club that my brother mentioned. It's another thing which I'm sure isn't good for Diana—and all this crazy stuff when combined together has, I think, just led to her starting to suffer from anxiety and being haunted by hallucinations. Her drinking came after that, I believe, as an attempt to cope with the anxiety, to drive away the horrible images ... but it has just made everything worse."

"What's this club all about?" asked Victoria. "Is it some kind of secret society?"

"No, no, nothing so dramatic. Call it a reading circle, where nothing but horror literature is ever read. There are only a handful of members, mostly from the family circle, plus a few neighbors—and we just get together every Wednesday to read stories about ghosts, vampires, demons and the like. Actually a harmless pastime, one would think. Nowadays, movie theaters show worse things to fourteen-year-olds. But it seems to be poison for Diana."

"I guess the club alone can't really be to blame for Diana's problems," Bastian said in a somewhat more conciliatory tone. "You're probably right about that. But if you put it together with everything else—Juno's illness, and Barbara the old hag, in whose eyes no one could ever be good enough—it just eats Diana up. She's no supermom, at least not the kind Barbara would like to see."

"Barbara is Diana's late husband's older sister," Sendrik explained, "and therefore Juno's aunt. And well, she almost smothers the child with her love."

"Love? Pah!" Bastian exclaimed. "More like an obsession! She needs a shrink, too, if you ask me!"

He bit his lips and gave Victoria a guilty look. "I'm sorry, doctor, I didn't mean it that way. I really don't have anything against psychology, honestly, or even against you."

Our human forced herself to smile. "That's all right," she said.

"Shall we go downstairs, Victoria?" Sendrik suggested. "For a drink, or a cup of tea? And while we're at it, I'll introduce you to the other residents of the house."

Victoria agreed, and we all walked together down the wide, boldly-curved staircase to the ground floor.

The steps were so high that Pearl could only descend them by hopping from one down to the next—somehow reminding me of a rabbit. *Hippity hoppity.*

Of course I didn't tell her that, because I didn't want to suffer a scratched nose.

5

The house's occupants—and two guests—had gathered on the ground floor of the castle, in a kind of salon furnished in the Alpine style. Here lighter wood was to be found, less-gloomy carpets and curtains, and on the walls some paintings with mountain motifs, chamois and eagles.

The narrow side of the room consisted of a stone wall without plaster, in which a large open fireplace was set. The floor was built of rough wooden planks, covered by silky soft carpets. They felt fantastic under my paws.

Above our heads hung two mighty crystal chandeliers that didn't seem to me to quite fit the Alpine style. But what do I know? A dog is not an interior designer, after all.

Despite its considerable size the room seemed quite cozy, or at least less eerie than other parts of the castle, and it had large glass French doors through which one could go out onto a terrace. They were standing open to let in the evening air, which was still quite warm. Only the coolness of the old walls made the temperature in the room bearable at all.

I immediately set about inspecting the terrace, even before I sniffed the two-leggeds present in the room. But when I ran out into the open air, I caught my breath.

The terrace was made entirely of glass—that is, except for a few steel beams that formed the supporting structure and the railing. Both the floor and the walls were transparent.

We were now on the back side of the manor, which I had not yet been able to look at since we'd arrived. Here the terrain did not slope gradually down toward the valley, but rather plunged abruptly over rocky cliffs into a ravine. Between the house and the abyss there was just a narrow ridge, a mere couple of meters wide—and on this the terrace was set. Behind the glass railing only the evening sky could be seen, and in the distance were the surrounding mountain peaks.

I heard an eerie rushing sound beneath my paws, and as I peered into the depths I saw that a waterfall was cascading down into the gorge. It leaped over jagged rocks into the abyss, hissing and foaming like Pearl when she was in a terrible mood. What a place to build a house!

But perhaps I should move on to describing the people present in the room; people are endlessly more exciting than any waterfall or ravine, no matter how deep, aren't they?

First, I made the acquaintance of Juno, who was lying wrapped in a blanket on one of the sofas. Pearl greeted her with a cuddle, as she had already done with Diana, and conquered another human heart in no time.

Juno uttered the usual sounds of delight—"Oh my gosh, she's so cute!"—and so on.

At least she also cuddled my head afterwards, and

when she finally shook Victoria's hand in greeting, she complimented her on her 'awesome pets.' Victoria accepted the tribute with a smile.

Next to Juno sat a man with blond curls, whom she introduced as her boyfriend, Daniel Kirsch. Juno was still a teenager, not yet sixteen years old, as her mother had already told us. She was incredibly thin, with bones protruding from her shoulders and cheeks, arms and hands. Her hair was almost black, her eyes gray-brown, and her lips so bloodless that they barely stood out against the skin of her face. A bitter medicinal smell emanated from the girl.

Her boyfriend Daniel—well, he was at least twice Juno's age, maybe even in his early forties.

Unusual.

It didn't escape me that Victoria's eyes had widened in surprise at the sight of him. She was too tactful to make any remark, but even so, she must have been taken aback by Daniel's appearance, which was in almost painful contrast to that of his girlfriend. He was vigorously healthy, muscularly built, and had sun-bleached streaks in his hair, as if he spent a lot of time on beaches or in swimming pools. He also had bright blue eyes and a dazzling smile.

A human version of Pearl, I thought to myself. *A heartbreaker*. Surely all women found him 'cute,' if not irresistible.

Two men sat at a table on the other side of the room, playing cards. Sendrik, who was showing Victoria around and introducing her to everyone, called them by name—at which point they both rose from their chairs.

"This is Chris Wieland, Juno's tutor," Sendrik introduced the younger of the two. "Here in Italy, home-schooling is legal, just as it is with you guys in Austria," he explained, "and we decided to go for it because of Juno's ... um, delicate health. She attended her first few classes in a nearby public school down in the valley, but she stayed home too often for health reasons and was constantly infected with all kinds of diseases by her classmates. Her immune system, unfortunately, is not—"

He hesitated, probably coming to the realization that now was not the time for a medical discussion of his stepdaughter.

"Mr. Wieland is a very capable teacher," he said instead, patting the young man on the back. "We are pleased with him all round. He is staying here with us at the castle, and will be teaching Juno until she is ready to graduate from high school. That way she'll be able to learn at her own pace, and the curriculum will be tailor-made for her. After that..."

Again he broke off abruptly. "Well, it's written in the stars, I'm afraid." His expression darkened, and he added nothing more.

As a doctor, did he already know how bad things really were for Juno? That perhaps it made no sense at all to make longer-term plans for the future?

If I could trust my nose, the girl was in very bad shape. She smelled like the sort of person who suffers from all kinds of diseases and usually has only weeks or months to live. But Juno was still so young! I felt sorry for the poor girl.

"Juno is a brilliant student," Chris Wieland said as he gently shook Victoria's hand. I liked him right away. He had kind eyes, a thick brown beard, and a pleasant voice.

"And this is our newest guest, Rolf Bachmann, MD," Sendrik introduced the second of the two card players. He added no words of praise for him as he had done with Chris Wieland.

Dr. Bachmann was very small for a grown man, still quite young for a doctor, and he had strangely pointed canines that made me suddenly think of a vampire. Who could blame me, in this eerie Dracula castle we had landed in!

Then a maid came rushing over and asked Victoria for her drink request.

She ordered black tea with milk on the side and took a seat together with Sendrik on another sofa, which stood directly in front of the open fireplace and a bit away from the other two-leggeds. He also asked the maid to bring him a cup of tea.

"Juno's boyfriend," Victoria began in a whisper, after the steaming hot drinks had been served, "he's, how shall I put it—"

She couldn't seem to find the right words. Embarrassed, she added milk and sugar to her tea and then stirred thoroughly. The china was black with golden edges, and had a dark red floral pattern.

Sendrik helped her out with a wry smile. "Clearly too old, you mean? He's old enough to be Juno's father?"

Victoria grinned back, embarrassed. "Well, maybe I'm terribly bourgeois, but he does seem a little—how shall I say it—too mature compared to her?"

Sendrik shrugged. "The ways of love are passing strange. Isn't that what they say? He's sort of a neighbor, you know; his house is a little further down the valley. That's how the two of them met. Poor Juno doesn't often get to go into town or to other places where she might meet people her own age, unfortunately."

"And he looks like a frigging model, too," Victoria added, lost in thought.

Sendrik's smile widened. "But it does seem to me that he's really devoted to Juno. They're already talking seriously about getting married. Juno will soon be sixteen, and by then she will legally be allowed to tie the knot. Barbara, of course, is beside herself at the mere idea; you can imagine, I'm sure. She probably prefers the idea of Juno ending up as an old maid."

"And how do you feel about it, Sendrik?" Victoria asked.

His smile vanished. "I do want Juno to have fun, from the bottom of my heart, even if to be honest I personally think it's a bit early for marriage. But I can't and won't tell her what to do. I am only her stepfather, even if I don't love her one bit less because of it. All I

38

care about is that Daniel doesn't break her heart. Perhaps you, as a psychologist, could scrutinize him for me—put him to the acid test, so to speak, to find out if he's genuine?"

"Oh, it would be great," Victoria promptly replied, "if you could see inside people in such a way that you always knew exactly where you stood. But it doesn't work, I'm afraid. Not even if you've studied psychology."

"What a shame," Sendrik said.

A short pause arose. Out of the corner of my eye I could see that Pearl, who had made herself comfortable on Victoria's lap, was already dozing off.

Victoria rumpled her neck, then addressed Sendrik again: "Dr. Bachmann—is he a colleague of yours? I noticed you were very tight-lipped when you introduced him to me."

Sendrik sipped his tea, and once again the corners of his mouth twisted into a wry smile. "You may claim not to be able to see inside people, Victoria, but you do seem to me to be a very keen observer. I hope I wasn't too rude; far be it from me to offend my colleague Bachmann. He is a capable young doctor."

"But is he a specialist you called in because of Juno's health condition? She does seem very ill, if I may say so. Poor girl—what's wrong with her, anyway?"

Sendrik put down his teacup, but held it for a moment as if he needed to warm his soul with it.

"Bachmann is a general practitioner, not a specialist. We—or rather Diana and her first husband, Alexander—have already been to see various specialists with Juno. It is difficult to determine what exactly is wrong with her; everything and nothing, you could say, even though that may sound very like a layman. Her immune system is not working properly, and lately her metabolism is spinning out of control as well. She is getting weaker and weaker ... and I am simply powerless against it, although I have really tried everything I can think of. Unfortunately some children are just born with a very weak constitution. But as for my colleague Bachmann—he was summoned by Barbara. She doesn't think I'm a good enough doctor."

He furrowed his brow. "Barbara doesn't have any children of her own, you know. And she's really obsessed with Juno, as my brother has already said quite correctly. It's not at all healthy, if you ask me."

He shook his head. "To get back to Dr. Bachmann: he's only been with us for a few days, but he's going to stay for a couple more weeks in order to run all kinds of tests on Juno. He'll observe her routines, and keep a close record of her vital signs, diet and so on. Nothing I haven't done already myself, but of course I still hope he'll succeed where I have failed."

6

As if she had heard her name telepathically and rushed over, Barbara entered the salon at that moment.

She stopped briefly on the threshold, looked over at us, but then walked to the sofa where Juno and Daniel had made themselves comfortable.

I strained my ears to hear her words.

She bent over the girl and whispered softly but firmly, "Time to go to sleep, my child."

Turning to Daniel—and in a far less tender tone— she added: "You shouldn't be here, Mr. Kirsch. Don't you know how late it is already—and that Juno needs her sleep?"

At that moment, Chris Wieland, the tutor who was still playing cards with Dr. Bachmann, turned to Juno. Apparently he had overheard the aunt's admonition.

"Tomorrow we'll write a math paper. I hope you haven't forgotten, huh?" he reminded his student. His tone was serious but still very friendly.

"I haven't, Mr. Wieland," Juno said meekly.

She crawled out from under her blanket and got to her feet with difficulty, like an elderly woman, standing there quite shakily. She gave Daniel a shy kiss on the cheek and, leaning on Barbara's arm, left the room.

When the door had closed behind her, Victoria

turned back to Sendrik. "Can you tell me a little more about the hallucinations that are haunting Diana, please? You mentioned the noises tonight, the werewolf rattling—or what is it that she called it?"

Sendrik nodded. "The werewolf thing is a new one. In recent weeks Diana had been dreaming, or should I say hallucinating, mostly about vampires. Once she woke up screaming in the middle of the night, insisting that someone had invaded her room and drawn her blood with the help of a hypodermic needle ... which seems somehow too modern for a vampire, don't you think? Not to mention the sheer absurdity of such an idea. Another time she claimed to have heard the fluttering of bats in her room, and once blood was even found on her pillow when she'd had another nightmare."

"Blood?" Victoria asked. "That does seem quite concrete to me, and not a mere delusion. That is, if you saw it too."

"I did. It was on her pillow. I assumed she'd had a nosebleed and tried to calm her down with that explanation. But she insisted that a vampire was pursuing her. And in the weeks before that, before the vampires, she was terrified that a ghost was stalking her. And those were the exact themes of the Wednesday Evening Club at the respective times, you see. Each week a different member reads a story or sample from a novel, which the other participants can then continue to read on their own, if they so wish. In the process we often stay with the same theme for a couple of weeks. It just comes up, you know—it's not a hard and fast rule. If one person introduces a good vampire story, the next member wants to present one as well. That's kind of how it goes. Last week it was my turn to be the reader again, and I deliberately left the vampires behind. I read a werewolf story, hoping that Diana would then stop fantasizing about those bloodsuckers."

"But now she hears werewolf noises instead," Victoria said.

Sendrik sighed. "Yes, unfortunately. What do you think—this thematic connection between the reading material at the club and Diana's nightmares or hallucinations—doesn't that indicate that these stories could be the cause?"

"Quite possibly," Victoria confirmed.

Sendrik nodded, looking frustrated. "She won't stay away from the club meetings no matter the cost. It's mostly because of Juno, because she loves the club more than anything else and doesn't have many other opportunities to enjoy herself. She simply doesn't have the energy for the usual teenage activities, like the cinema, disco evenings, sports and so on. Even when she's not acutely struggling with a new bout of illness."

He ran his hand through his dark hair and reached for his teacup again.

"It's really awful," he muttered. "First Juno, and now Diana is in such a bad way. I don't know what to do anymore. Where is it all going to end, I ask you?"

Later, when Victoria had gone to bed, Pearl and I waited until she fell asleep. Then we decided to roam around the castle a bit to explore.

Fortunately, the door handle was one that you merely had to push down to open. No obstacle for me.

Pearl and I crept out into the hallway, which was in darkness. But there was still a faint glow of light under the door leading to Diana's bedroom. After the sedative had done its work, had she woken up again? Was she all right?

I ran toward the strip of light, and Pearl followed me on quiet paws. Before we'd even reached the door, we realized that Diana must indeed be awake—and that she was not alone in the room. Her voice, and that of another, drifted out to us in the hallway.

Diana seemed to be very agitated again, but this time it was not a werewolf's fault. Rather, she was arguing with a two-legged. It was a man whose voice was already familiar to me: Bastian, Sendrik's brother. His smoky aroma again wafted in the air. I could even sniff it through the narrow gap under the door. The door was carpentered from thick wood and strongly muffled the argument in the bedroom. But with dog or cat ears, fortunately, you could still understand what the heated discussion was all about.

"Let me finally take you away from here, Diana!" Bastian cried with fervor. "I beg you! This morbid old castle just isn't healthy for you, you must face it. And Sendrik doesn't appreciate you at all!"

Pearl and I looked at each other in astonishment.

What was going on here?

Diana's answer came just as heatedly: "This castle is Juno's home, and I will certainly not abandon her! And it was the ancestral home of my late husband."

"Whom you are still crying after!" Bastian reproached her.

"So what? What's it to you?"

Bastian shifted to a somewhat gentler approach: "I'm sure a less morbid atmosphere would be good for Juno, too," he implored Diana. "I can offer you both whatever you desire. My hotels are doing fantastically well, and I'll be bringing in record profits again this year..."

"If you're as rich as you always claim, then maybe you should finally buy your own house instead of living here with us!" Diana snapped, cutting him off.

"That's really unfair, my dear! You know exactly why I live here. Only to be near to you!"

For a moment there was silence. I'd already assumed that this strange argument was now over, but then Diana's voice could be heard again: "I can't believe you really want to steal your own brother's wife, Bastian!"

He promptly replied, "Sendrik doesn't deserve you, Diana. And you're powerless against my love, I'm sure I don't have to tell you that. You do love me, don't you? Admit it! Our night together..."

"...was a mistake, Bastian!" she interrupted him, her voice almost breaking. "A *one-time* misstep that I certainly won't repeat! Now please let me sleep. I'm dog-tired!"

Again there was a small pause, but the door did not

open as I was expecting. Instead, Bastian said, quieter now, no longer so passionate, but audibly gripped by a cold anger: "I could tell Sendrik about our night together. For your sake, Diana, so he'd leave you and we could finally be together. I'm sure you'd thank me for it in the end."

"Get out of here, you *monster*," Diana screamed hysterically, and then something banged against the wall.

Pearl jumped, startled, even though of course we weren't in the line of fire here in the hallway. Apparently Diana had thrown some object at Bastian and missed. The impact had sounded like masonry, not a human skull.

"If you try to destroy my family, I'll kill you!" Diana roared.

Another object crashed against the wall—and then the door flew open and Bastian came storming out of the room.

I couldn't get out of his way fast enough. He tripped over me, stumbled and hit the ground hard.

With a curse that must have been directed equally at me and at Diana, he got back to his feet, gasped, and finally disappeared with a limp toward the smaller stairwell that lay at the far end of the corridor.

"Do you think Sendrik might have overheard all of this?" Pearl asked me.

We took a look under his bedroom door, but the room was dark and we could not hear the slightest sound.

"Let's go see. Maybe he's still down in the parlor," I

suggested.

And indeed we found him there. He had joined Chris Wieland and Dr. Bachmann's card game—and thus could not have heard what had transpired in his wife's bedroom.

7

Victoria spent Tuesday and most of Wednesday in endless conversation with Diana. She kept asking her new questions and listening attentively, and it seemed to me that she had succeeded, at least to some extent, in alleviating her client's fears.

At first I followed the sessions, but I must confess that at some point I preferred to find a shady spot in the garden—with a stunning view of the mountain peaks—and dozed off for a bit. After all, we were on vacation, apart from Victoria's work with Diana.

Pearl roamed around, but stayed in my line of sight without my having to prompt her. Above us in the cloudless sky birds of prey of various species were frolicking, and up here in the solitude of the mountains it was also impossible to predict which quadrupeds might be prowling near us. All creatures that might see a juicy and easily earned snack in a dwarf-sized, completely defenseless housecat.

On Wednesday afternoon, Pearl sat for hours on the narrow ridge between the castle and the waterfall, staring down in fascination at a pair of chamois who were romping about on an almost vertical mountain face to the left of the cascade. They seemed to frolic there as I would in a freshly snow-covered field, carefree and happy, without a single thought of danger. The fact that a single misstep could mean their certain death did not seem to instill any fear in them.

At some point I left Pearl to herself and her contemplations of the wildlife—of course not without warning her to occasionally let her gaze wander in the direction of the sky to see if she herself was not being observed from up there. As always she replied that she could take care of herself and certainly didn't need a canine bodyguard.

I returned to the house and continued the tour I had started on the first night.

I visited the countless rooms of the castle, from the ground floor to the roof. Dark woods and wall colorings dominated everywhere, and even the carpets that covered large parts of the floors had an eerie feel to them. Their mostly red tones reminded me of blood, but that might just have been because the rest of the furnishings could have come from a chamber of horrors.

The corridors were filled with portraits of ancestors, none of whom ever seemed to smile, and with gloomy landscape paintings that spread a sort of doomsday mood. How could anyone voluntarily live in such a very gothic castle?

Pearl returned to the house before dinner, but declined my suggestion that a nap together in a quiet and cool corner of the castle would be nice.

"Need to do something in the kitchen," she told me cryptically, striding right past me on her tiny paws. Of course I followed her instead of indulging in a siesta alone. What was the midget up to now?

I should have known. Her visit to the kitchen was for something very obvious: our food while we were guests at the castle. As I mentioned earlier, Victoria had only brought dry food for us on the trip, and Pearl had no intention of settling for that. So her plan was to enter the kitchen and win the cook's heart.

To our astonishment, though, the castle cook was not a woman at all, as we would normally have expected, but a young lanky guy named Francesco. And he was allergic to cats! It was hilarious the way he tried to make that clear to Pearl in the midst of a sneezing fit, only to drive her out of his realm with almost hysterical words and rather rude gestures.

Meowing miserably, she zoomed out into the corridor. I, on the other hand, was not only permitted to stay, but even treated as an honored guest.

Francesco must have liked dogs, especially big and comely ones like me. Forgetting his work at the big kitchen range, he instead went down on his knees next to me and scratched first my neck and then my ears.

Finally he asked, "Well, sweetie, are you hungry by any chance?"

I squinted in the direction of the door, which was still open, and saw Pearl sitting outside in the hallway like a frozen stone statue. She said nothing, just eyed me silently, but I could tell she was seething with anger inside.

Panting, and with an encouraging yelp, I let Francesco know that a little snack was always a good idea—whereupon he walked over to the refrigerator, fetched a plate from one of the china cabinets and finally put a large piece of a chicken pie in front of me. It tasted quite delicious.

I have to admit that I may have deliberately taken my time eating it so as to annoy Pearl a bit. But since I am a very kind dog, I finally grabbed the last piece of pie and took it to her.

The cook had no objection to this; on the contrary, he called after me with delight at what a good-natured fellow I was, and how cute he found my interspecies friendship with Pearl.

In a nutshell, we had found an ally in the house who was to spoil us frequently with culinary delights over the next few days.

After the humans' dinner, we and Victoria finally made our way to the library—where the weekly meeting of the Wednesday Evening Club was to be held—and I was very grateful to have had a good meal. After all, what awaited us there could have upset the stomach of even the most fearless sled dog.

At first everything began quite harmlessly—as is often the case with even the scariest stories.

The room itself was finished in heavy black wood, as one might expect given the rest of the castle, and the bookshelves that lined all the walls were full to bursting.

The Messners—and now the Leonhardts—were apparently obsessive book lovers. I assumed that most of the works were chiller novels and horror stories. I couldn't read the titles, of course, but the pictures on some of the book covers that were visible confirmed my assumption.

Every castle resident had gathered in the library. They had all settled down on comfortable sofas and armchairs arranged in a large circle in the center of the room; a reading circle in the truest sense of the word.

Diana, smelling strongly of alcohol again tonight—at least to my dog's nose—sat down beside Victoria; right next to her Juno was lounging under a blanket on a sofa, with her boyfriend Daniel by her side. She seemed to be really looking forward to the club tonight. Her cheeks were slightly flushed, and her eyes shone brightly with expectation.

To my surprise, Barbara Messner looked similarly excited. She was sitting next to the tutor, Chris, and looked years younger than before. And much friendlier. She also seemed to be looking forward to this evening of horror in joyful anticipation.

Sendrik and Bastian Leonhardt were present as well, along with the guest physician, Dr. Bachmann, and finally another man whom I had not seen in the castle up to that point.

The Leonhardts addressed him as Thiele, though I wasn't quite sure if that was his first or family name. He was quite an old codger, with a tangled mop of hair and coarse black shoes.

He had apparently tried to dress up for the night, even though the suit he was wearing already looked pretty worn. The unpleasant smell of mothballs drifted toward my nostrils.

Diana introduced Thiele to Victoria, referring to him as 'our immediate neighbor and longtime honorary family member.'

"He was friends with my late husband for many years," Diana said, "and in his younger years he was a hiking guide here in the area. He knows the mountains like the back of his hand. Now he's retired and lives in our gatehouse, and he's an enthusiastic member of our Wednesday Evening Club, aren't you, Thiele? And by now the longest-standing one—a real connoisseur of Gothic literature."

The old man grunted and acknowledged Diana's praise with a shy smile, exposing dazzling white teeth that were certainly not real.

Next, Diana launched into a welcome to the new-comers: "We are pleased to welcome you, Victoria, and you, Dr. Bachmann, as guest members of the Wednes-day Evening Club," she announced. *"May you be pleas-antly creeped out, and may your sleepless nights be filled with exciting stories*—this is how we traditionally welcome new readers to our circle."

She tried to smile at her words, but failed. It was quite obvious that she couldn't associate the term *creeped out* with anything pleasant at all—nor the idea of sleepless nights. She had probably had too many of those lately, and must have found herself in a state of mind in which she couldn't even think of comfortable reading hours.

She added a brief history of the club, recounting how it had been in existence for over a hundred years, and that the Messner family had not missed a single Wednesday evening over that period—no matter whether there was a war going on in the world, a new government was being elected, or if the family itself was beset by strokes of fate.

Allegedly even some of the poets, whose horror stories were read with such pleasure at the club, had visited the castle themselves and attended meetings as guest members.

While a maid served drinks and nibbles to the two-legged guests, I tried to find a spot in front of one of the shelf walls from where I would have a good view of the room.

No sooner said than done: I let myself fall on my belly in front of one of the bookshelves a short distance from Pearl, who was lying closer to the humans, and was about to put my head on my paws to be as comfortable as possible and listen to the scary story of the day. I like it when people read something aloud, even though I very rarely get to enjoy it. Mostly I just follow stories on a TV screen.

In principle nothing could stand in the way of a wonderful evening, but just as I was stretching out comfortably one of the books fell from the shelf—right onto my head. Fortunately it was only a slim paperback, not a hardcover with a thousand pages, but the impact was still quite painful.

I let out a startled yelp. How could a book have just fallen off the shelf like that? The cabinets were packed, but not so much so that any of the books were in danger of falling off.

A few of the two-leggeds turned to look at me in surprise. I got up on my paws, walked a few steps, and then settled down again.

As a sled dog I really wouldn't call myself sensitive to drafts, or even to cold temperatures, but no sooner had I lowered my head onto my paws again than an ice-cold breeze swept over my back.

"Damn it," I growled, though of course only Pearl could understand me.

"What's the matter?" she asked. She herself, who usually felt cold much faster than I did and hated drafts with a vengeance, was lying comfortably in her spot and seemed to be perfectly at ease.

"I don't know," I muttered. "There's a draft in here! Don't tell me you can't feel it?"

"Nope," said Pearl.

At that moment, a second book fell on my head.

8

I yelped and jumped up angrily.

"Hey, check this out," Juno exclaimed. "It must be our castle ghost! From the looks of it, Athos has scared her, and she's throwing books at him. I guess she doesn't like dogs."

Diana let out a nervous laugh.

Daniel patted Juno's hand. "Don't they say that *cats* can sense the supernatural?" he mused.

"I've heard that somewhere, too," Juno said.

She straightened up on her sofa and peered intently at me, as if she wanted to stare holes through my head. Then she let her gaze wander and searched my immediate surroundings with her eyes, and finally glanced at Pearl.

"Well, you two," she said, "can you see her—our library spirit?"

"Nobody's seen it in generations!" old Thiele interjected. "Can we finally start reading now?"

"Well, I do get the impression sometimes that she hangs around the castle," Juno objected. "Especially here in the library. I can't see her or hear her, but I think I can sense her presence sometimes—only when I'm alone, never in the company of other people. Maybe she's quite shy?"

"Pah, such nonsense," the old man said gruffly. Either he was just in a bad mood, or he was trying to compete with Barbara Messner in terms of surliness. In any case, Juno earned a very disapproving look from him.

Sendrik, on the other hand, turned questioningly to his stepdaughter. "*She,* you say. So you believe this ghost is a woman?" He spoke lightly, not really seeming to take the matter seriously.

Juno nodded eagerly, which ended in a coughing fit. Daniel put his arm around her shoulders protectively.

"Shhhh, dear, take it easy." He gently patted her back as if he could thereby drive away the coughing fit.

I saw the guest physician, Dr. Bachmann, grimace. In his eyes this was apparently not an appropriate measure to help the girl. However, he refrained from intervening himself.

When Juno finally got her breath back, she said—this time without abruptly moving her head—"Yes, I think the ghost is a *she*. And I think she likes our books; that's why she hangs out here in the library. Father never saw her himself, you know, but he told me that from the middle of the twentieth century she is said to have haunted this room. And she was supposedly throwing books around even then!"

"Can you sense anything?" I asked Pearl. "Is it true that cats can see ghosts?"

I received an uncertain look.

"I don't know," the tiny one said. "I've never heard of that before. Do ghosts even exist?"

She looked around, a little afraid it seemed to me, and sniffed. However she did not seem to perceive anything out of the ordinary.

Victoria gave Juno an attentive look, while Diana rebuked her daughter—kindly yet firmly, or rather anxiously, for she suddenly smelled of fear. "Don't give me that nonsense, honey! Ghosts only exist in books, you know that!"

"Is Diana afraid her daughter might also have *hallunications* like she does herself?" Pearl asked me.

"Hallucinations," I corrected her. "Quite possibly. Some mental illnesses are hereditary; I've heard Victoria say that before."

"Can we finally start now, please?" old Thiele nagged again.

This time his wish was granted.

Today it was apparently Daniel's turn to read a story. He took a thick book with a gloomy-looking cover from the side table to his left and opened it.

I made a third attempt to find a comfortable place to listen. This time I walked over to the other side of the room and lay down behind two armchairs, where Barbara the dragon and Chris the tutor were sitting.

At least no book fell on my head this time—which might have been because I was keeping a safe distance from the shelves. But as soon as I had settled down another icy breeze swept over me.

I growled softly. I didn't want to attract the attention of the two-leggeds again, but on the other hand I couldn't believe that there was really such a terrible draft in this library. The windows and terrace doors of the room were closed and locked, as was the door into the hallway as well.

So I decided to ignore the cold. After all, I am a Malamute and have a coat that could take on ice and snow and the worst winter storms!

I lay down, but I had already missed Daniel's first words, which immediately annoyed me even more. After all, the beginning of a story is very important if you want to know your way around subsequent plot points.

When watching TV, it happened to me embarrassingly often that I fell asleep in the middle of a movie and so missed crucial scenes. But here and now, while a two-legged was reading live and I wasn't tired at all, I didn't want to miss anything. So I bravely ignored the icy air that was seemingly enveloping me like an ominous cloud and tried to listen to Daniel's words.

I did not succeed—because the cold suddenly seemed to change into something else, something evil, it seemed to me. A hostile presence that let me know in no uncertain terms that I was not welcome here in the library.

Was I already losing my mind in the strange atmosphere of this haunted castle? Would I end up like Diana, going mad and perhaps even needing a dog therapist in the end?

The next thing I knew, Daniel had paused in his reading of the story; apparently some time had passed.

People stood up and stretched their legs, and Bastian opened the terrace doors and went outside. The air that flowed into the room was warm and summery by comparison.

Drinks and snacks were being served again, and Pearl came sauntering over to me.

"Exciting story, huh?" she said casually.

She eyed the snack trays curiously, but they contained only potato chips, popcorn and nuts. Not the kind of delicacies my spoiled little gourmet cat liked to eat.

Barbara and Chris remained seated in their fauteuils, both drinking a cup of tea—which seemed appropriate considering the old building we were in, even if it stood in Italy and not in England.

Then, just as Daniel was adjusting a footstool for his sweetheart and placing a potato chip into her mouth with an amorous look, Barbara clicked her tongue in disapproval.

"What a farce he's putting on!" she hissed at the tutor, probably just quietly enough that none of the other two-leggeds in the room could hear her. "Who does he think he's trying to fool? Isn't it obvious that this gold digger is just after Juno's money?"

"*Money*?" Pearl repeated, catching Barbara's hateful words. "Juno has money? She's still so young, isn't she?"

"She probably inherited it from her father," I explained to the pipsqueak—and felt pretty smart in doing so.

"I don't trust Daniel either," Chris whispered to Barbara. "He's got a reputation around here as a good-for-nothing, a bon vivant ... and a ladies' man to boot. Besides, he's way too old for our Juno, isn't he?"

But that's as far as they got with their unflattering discussion of Daniel, for at that moment the pause came to an end and he reached for his book again.

This time I actually managed to concentrate on the story for the most part, but what I heard did not necessarily contribute to my relaxation.

The story, whose beginnings I'd missed, was apparently about an unhappy man who turned into a werewolf at night, every month during the full moon. However, he had—in his human phase—fallen madly in love with a young maid whose life he increasingly threatened with his transformations.

In the end, tragedy struck. The man—in a panic that in his wolf form he might bite to death the woman he loved—saw no way out. Just as the full moon was cresting the horizon once again, he threw himself over a steep cliff into the sea and found a watery grave there.

Humans are a really paradoxical species, I mused to myself. On the one hand, they are so helpless, emotionally unstable, practically blind and deaf ... not to mention their terrible sense of smell.

But they are also capable of truly heroic deeds when they love someone—as this story proved once again. The two-leggeds do crazy, great but also heinous things out of love.

I fell into a strange melancholy, musing on the ways of the heart. I myself loved Victoria, and the midget too, though of course I would never have admitted it to her. I enjoyed their company and my life with them, even though it was clearly peppered with too many dead bodies.

But a female Malamute? That would be something else entirely. Apart from my mother and a few sisters, whom I could barely remember, I had never met one. But surely there had to be many of them.

Was there perhaps a great love waiting for me with her, this unknown stranger? Would I, in order to save her, also voluntarily go to my death some time in the distant future, just like the werewolf in Daniel's story?

Then I would rather do without a great love, I said to myself.

Because of these strange and even morbid thoughts, for which the eerie castle with its flying books and cold drafts was certainly to blame, I unfortunately missed the end of the story. Daniel read a bit further, but I no longer heard his words.

What happened to the werewolf's beloved?

I would never know, for already a new, even darker thought took possession of me: what if I, as a dog closely related to actual wolves, were bitten by a werewolf? Would I then, always at full moon, change into a human being?

What a terrible thought.

9

Late that night I lay with Pearl on the terrace outside of Victoria's guest suite, which had a breathtaking view of the gorge.

The waterfall was rushing down over the rocks in a wild rhythm, a brilliant canopy of stars was stretched above our heads, and a pleasant wind had sprung up to dispel the heat of the day. Pearl was sleeping peacefully on my front paw, while Victoria was on a video call with her boyfriend Tim in the bedroom.

A few of their words penetrated my consciousness, which was still being haunted by werewolves.

Tim spoke remarkably little about his entrepreneurship course, so I gathered he wasn't really enjoying it much. But far more importantly, both he and Victoria sounded very much in love. That was good; Victoria seemed far more joyful now that Tim was part of her life, and after all, as a pet you are responsible for your two-legged's happiness. Pearl and I had done a good job.

As I, too, was slowly being overcome by sleep, a piercing howl suddenly tore me from my blissful state.

I immediately got to my paws, perhaps pushing Pearl aside a little ungently.

She complained with a sleepy hiss. "Sup?" she grumbled.

"Hush, can't you hear it?" I pricked up my ears, but

there was no need; the howling seemed to be coming from very close by.

"Wolves!" I exclaimed excitedly, "and a really big pack, too!"

I counted five, six, then nearly a dozen different voices joining in the howling. They seemed to have gathered somewhere to our left, in the immediate vicinity of the castle. No, wait, the howling was apparently coming from above—but that wasn't possible. Above us were only the second floor, the roof, and the night sky.

I stared into the darkness, first to the left, then upwards, but in both directions there were only other rooms of the castle, whose windows were no longer illuminated at this late hour. No trace of any wolves—and it's well known that they don't climb on people's buildings.

"Didn't know there were large wolf packs in these parts," Pearl meowed, already wanting to curl up and go to sleep again. But then suddenly her tiny ears perked up as well.

She gave me a questioning look. "What's wrong with them? Are they confused, or what?"

It was clear to me what she was alluding to—because the conversation the wolves were having was strange to say the least.

The leader of the pack was distributing orders for a reindeer hunt, which the wolves were going to start as soon as night fell.

"If we can even find specimens that haven't frozen to

death," one wolf commented.

"It's really one of the toughest winters in living memory," another animal—presumably an older one—chimed in.

"So what?" a defiant younger voice interjected, probably trying to exude some optimism. "It's not like all the reindeer will have died already. And they're weakened because they can hardly find food in all this snow..."

Something was very wrong here. *Reindeer*—in *South Tyrol*?

I had always been aware of the fact that these mighty hoofed animals, which I only knew from television, lived exclusively in the far north.

And was the hunt for them to begin as soon as night fell? It had long been night—a balmy summer night; there was no question of snow or freezing cold.

I tried again to locate the howling. It had stopped for a moment, but then suddenly started again. It definitely seemed to be coming from above. One could almost have thought that the wolves were sitting on the roof.

But what was that? Suddenly I was hearing different voices, which certainly did not belong to the same animals that had just planned their winter reindeer hunt.

This time there were only four or five wolves to be heard, and now suddenly there was talk of a mountain lion that had already killed several of the pack's cubs and therefore had to be eliminated urgently.

"Mountain lions? Reindeer?" said Pearl. "Have they

gone mad?"

At that very moment Diana stepped out onto the terrace to our left, which must belong to her bedroom. The terrace doors were open, so she couldn't possibly have missed the howling. Probably it had even lured her outside. She was wearing a floor-length white nightgown that was fluttering in the wind and made her look like a ghost herself.

She groped her way around anxiously, first looking up, then to the left, and finally over to us. But she didn't seem to notice us at all. There was naked fear in her eyes—was she wondering if the wolf howls were a new hallucination?

"We can hear it too," I barked at her, but of course it was no use.

She clung to the railing, which was made of steel and enclosed large panes of glass like on all the castle's terraces. Through the glass in front of her—or the transparent floor at her feet, I couldn't see it clearly—she seemed to perceive something—something that had to be below her, that is, on the narrow ridge that separated the castle from the gorge and its waterfall.

She suddenly bounced back as if a gust of wind had knocked her off her feet, and let out a sharp scream.

The next moment she fainted—landing ungently on the terrace floor. The glass groaned, but was stable enough not to break.

"Come on, we have to help her!" I shouted to Pearl, but she was already sprinting off, back into Victoria's bedchamber, where she called out to our human to come along with loud meows.

I on the other hand headed straight for the door which led out into the corridor. I stood on my hind paws, braced my front legs against the wood and pressed the handle down with my muzzle. The door burst open.

Pearl and I rushed out into the hallway—and Victoria, for once, immediately understood that something was wrong. She probably hadn't noticed Diana's scream from her bed, especially since she'd still been talking to Tim.

But now I heard her come running out into the hallway after us, calling out, "Athos? Pearl? Wait up! What's the matter?"

We ran straight to Diana's door, which was only a short distance away. Pearl meowed and scratched at it, while I again took care of the handle. Fortunately it was not locked.

I looked around for Victoria before rushing into the room. Good, there were only a few steps ahead of her before she would reach us. At the same time, however, there were footsteps coming from the other side of the hall.

The next moment I realized who was responsible: Bastian Leonhardt came rushing down the back stairs from the second floor.

All together we stormed into Diana's room, with Bastian almost stepping on Pearl. Fortunately she managed to get out of harm's way with an impressive leap.

On the bedroom terrace Diana was just coming to

again. She pulled herself up heavily, leaning on the railing, stood there for a moment as if stuck, and stared at us unblinkingly.

But then she seemed to remember what had given her such a shock; she turned away from us and toward the abyss. Her hands clutched at the steel of the railing and she bent far over it. For a moment I thought she was about to throw herself into the depths.

Victoria probably had assumed something similar, because she took off running, overcoming the few steps that still separated her from her client and yelled, "Don't, Diana!"

But Diana didn't want to jump. She was just staring into the depths as if spellbound, and finally cried out in a shrill voice: "But that's impossible. I saw him! Down there—and now he's gone."

Victoria reached her, wrapped her arm around her waist, gazed into the abyss herself for a moment, and then pulled her friend off the terrace and back into the room.

Bastian probably also wanted to make himself useful. He quickly pushed a few books from off the sofa next to the terrace doors. "Here, Diana, sit down."

He spread his arms and let himself fall onto the couch—and Diana finally reacted as if in a trance. She didn't let go of Victoria, but pulled her with her onto the sofa. It was big enough to fit all three of them.

I ran out onto the terrace. I was dying to know what Diana had seen there.

But there was ... absolutely nothing?

I had a clear view through the glass floor, but I couldn't see anything in front of the house that would have justified fainting. There was only the narrow ridge that separated the castle from the abyss, and nothing else. Here, directly under Diana's balcony, it was a little wider than in front of other parts of the castle, covered with gravel and flanked by some shrubbery toward the precipice.

The strange wolf howl had long since died away. When I remembered it, a crazy thought suddenly popped into my head: what if the howling was not from ordinary wolves, but from *werewolves*? Maybe that explained the completely meaningless conversations. Reindeer, mountain lions, the icy winter night....

Had I in fact heard no close kindred of mine, but instead humans who had turned into wolves and therefore lost their minds?

I raised my eyes to the sky where hung an almost full moon. But werewolves are a product of the human imagination, I tried to tell myself. Only with moderate success.

I ran back into the room, where Pearl was already comforting Diana. For some reason, petting cats has a calming effect on most two-leggeds. I had observed this more than once, and Diana was no exception. She was sitting there with Pearl on her lap, stroking the tiny cat's head with such vigorous movements that it was sure to be giving her a headache. But Pearl bravely endured the treatment.

Victoria, meanwhile, was trying to get out of her client what had put her in such a state of shock.

"Dr. B-Bachmann," Diana finally stammered, after several unsuccessful attempts to utter a coherent sentence. "He was lying down there—under my balcony. He looked—dead. But he's gone now."

With a confused, fear-filled look, she clawed her nails into Victoria's arm, making her gasp.

Victoria, who'd looked down from the terrace just as I had, hadn't noticed anything conspicuous down there—certainly not a corpse. I could tell that from her face—and so could Diana as well, apparently.

"I told you, he's gone now!" she defended herself, without Victoria saying any accusing word to imply that the body had been merely a product of her imagination.

Uncertainly, Diana continued, "Didn't you hear the wolves earlier? Their howling tore me from my sleep. I ran out onto the terrace to—oh, I don't know what I hoped to see there, either. Or rather feared. I was thinking of the werewolf from tonight's story. I looked around outside, and that's when I discovered..."

She slapped her hands in front of her face and sobbed. "He was dead," she repeated in the tone of a possessed woman. "He was dead for sure."

"I heard the howling too, I think," Victoria said. "You weren't imagining it. I must confess, though, that I wasn't really paying attention. I was on the phone— and I thought to myself that Athos was just howling at the moon out on the terrace. He does that sometimes, you know. I guess he just thinks he's a wolf occasionally."

"Pffft!" I said to Pearl. "The way she says it, it sounds like I've got a screw loose."

"How come?" the pipsqueak replied. "You're always stressing how closely related you are to the wolves. And you do howl sometimes, don't you?"

Victoria turned, addressing Bastian: "Round everyone up, please. I'll stay with Diana in the meantime. Above all, see if you can find Dr. Bachmann—we need to determine if anything has indeed happened to him."

Bastian looked less than enthusiastic; he apparently didn't want to leave Diana, but finally gave in and jumped up. He left the room in a hurry.

10

Perhaps ten minutes passed before Bastian returned with Sendrik and Barbara in tow. Diana had calmed down a little in the meantime; Pearl's and Victoria's efforts had not failed to have an effect.

"What about Dr. Bachmann?" our human addressed Bastian with a questioning look. "Were you not able to find him?"

Bastian shook his head and then glanced at Barbara.

"Dr. Bachmann quit without notice," the old lady explained. "It appears he had to leave urgently because a regular patient needed his help. Something life-threatening, or so he said."

"When did you talk to him?" asked Victoria. "And when did he leave? It must be a very urgent case indeed if he disappeared so hastily in the middle of the night."

"We didn't speak in person," Barbara said stiffly. "He merely wrote me a short message half an hour ago. Very unusual behavior, I must say. He added that he didn't think he could help Juno anyway, but he promised to recommend a suitable colleague to me."

"I checked his room," Bastian said. "His luggage is gone."

"And his car?" Victoria asked.

Bastian shook his head. "He didn't come by car. He arrived by train and a cab from the station brought him here."

"Then he must have left the same way," Victoria said. "Did any of you see him leave? I myself was already in bed."

Everyone present shook their heads.

"Really appalling, such unreliability!" Barbara uttered severely. "To think that I was so mistaken about the man! I thought he was such an extremely upright person."

"Don't you think something might have happened to him?" Victoria asked. "After all, Diana saw him lying motionless in front of the house. He may not have been dead, so he could still have dragged himself away ... but maybe he is badly injured? Shouldn't we call the police to look for him?"

"Excellent," Pearl meowed to me. "Victoria is getting involved as a sleuth—she's asking questions. That's going in the right direction, don't you think?"

"Hmm, yeah," I mumbled absently.

My head was full of the wildest thoughts. What was going on here? What had happened to the doctor? Or had he truly left, and had Diana only imagined the sight of his body?

"Call the police?" Barbara remarked on our human's suggestion in a cutting voice. "That's out of the question. What would they think of us? Dr. Bachmann may have behaved inappropriately, just abandoning us like that, but that's not a crime after all."

She looked down at Diana, who was still sitting on the sofa, while she herself was standing wide-legged like a sergeant in front of her. Her gaze seemed to say: *you're really out of your mind if you think you've seen his body in front of this house.*

A brief discussion ensued among those present, but in the end it was agreed that the police were not needed.

Pearl meanwhile jumped off Diana's lap, shook herself, and then began to indulge in a grooming session on the floor. I looked once again in the direction of the terrace and happened to notice something at that moment. How could I have overlooked it earlier?

It was a small thing that lay to the right of the terrace door, and shimmered with gold. I walked up to it and realized that it was a button. One of the larger variety, the kind that two-leggeds wear on jackets rather than shirts or blouses. I gently took the button in my muzzle and brought it to Victoria.

She reached for it in amazement. "Where did you find that, Athos?"

I ran back to the terrace door to show her the spot.

She turned to Diana. "Is this yours, my dear?"

But Diana gave the button only a cursory glance. "No, definitely not."

Victoria frowned, but said nothing more. She let the button slide into the side pocket of the sleeveless vest she was wearing over her nightgown.

"I'm sure Dr. Bachmann was murdered," Pearl said to me as we made our way back to our bedroom, together with Victoria.

Sendrik had stayed with his wife; Barbara and Bastian also withdrew.

"Murdered? By whom?" I asked. "Diana didn't push him off the terrace. We would have seen that, wouldn't we?"

"Bastian could have done it," Pearl replied. "From his terrace, which is one floor up—or Sendrik from his, which is right next to Diana's—or someone could have bumped off Dr. Bachmann on the ground floor and then dumped his body outside. And maybe the murder happened much earlier, before Diana discovered the body and we weren't on the terrace to witness anything."

"How can the body have disappeared after Diana saw it under her balcony?"

"Hmm, it could have rolled away and fallen into the abyss?" Pearl suggested.

"Hardly," I said. "The area between the house and the ravine is not that narrow under Diana's balcony. And it's completely flat, not sloping. Nothing rolls away there on its own—especially not a dead person."

Pearl's nose twitched, making her whiskers vibrate, but she did not contradict me.

11

Back in bed, Victoria opened the laptop again and continued her video call with Tim. She began to describe the events to him.

"A death?" he said when she'd finished. "Do you think the doctor was murdered? Would you like me to join you at the castle? I can't believe you've gotten involved in another murder case."

"I don't know if it really was a murder," Victoria said quickly. "Or even if Dr. Bachmann is actually dead. Diana's sensory perceptions ... can't be thoroughly relied on, I'm afraid. It might all be quite harmless, in any event; Dr. Bachmann may indeed have left of his own accord. And no, you don't have to join me. It's sweet of you to suggest it, but you have your course to attend—that has priority. As I said, it will probably all blow over."

"For a doctor to just sneak out of the house without saying goodbye, merely leaving a quick message ... that does seem pretty strange," Tim said. "Although of course I don't know the guy."

"He certainly seemed like a completely competent and responsible doctor," Victoria said. "The message he supposedly left could have been sent by anyone who'd taken possession of his cell phone. And making his luggage disappear wouldn't be a problem, either."

Pearl purred contentedly. "What did I tell you,

Athos? She's really good. She has talent, she doesn't let anyone fool her, and she draws the right conclusions."

"Whether or not they're right, we don't know," I said, although of course I had to agree with Pearl; Victoria was doing quite well as a detective. I was worried that she might be putting herself in danger, however. If there really was a murderer at the castle...

"But I still can't imagine Dr. Bachmann being the victim of foul play," Victoria told Tim. "The thought is crazy, isn't it?"

"So your client really just imagined his dead body under her terrace?" Tim replied.

"That would be quite possible, I'm afraid," Victoria said. "She's not well at all, she suffers from panic attacks and hallucinations, and has an alcohol problem. On the other hand ... Athos found a button in Diana's room."

She squinted over at the little gold thing that she had set down on her nightstand. "I'm not one hundred percent sure, but I think Dr. Bachmann wore a jacket with gold buttons to dinner tonight."

"Oh my goodness, then he was in Diana's room?" said Tim. "What if there was a struggle, and the button came loose ... and then she threw him off the terrace? Would that be possible? Is the railing low enough—would she have the strength?"

"Tim loves to be a detective, too," I told Pearl.

"That's right," she returned proudly. "They make a good team."

"It's possible, I guess," Victoria was saying.

"Maybe Diana needed to shut the doctor up," Tim suggested eagerly. "Perhaps he found out something about her daughter—about Juno's illness. Something no one must know. So he had to die because of it."

"That's crazy, honey," Victoria countered. "Diana may have problems, but she's certainly no murderer. Besides, surely she wouldn't have screamed and had hysterics when she discovered the body … if she had murdered the man herself. She was beside herself with fear, I assure you."

"Maybe she's just a gifted actress. Or how about this: she has a split personality," Tim suggested. "You know, kind of like Dr. Jekyll and Mr. Hyde—one part of her has no idea what the other is doing. One is harmless, the other is a psychotic killer. One part of her kills the doctor, the other finds the body. Or rather, the other thinks she can still see the body, which in truth the psychotic part has long since disposed of."

"Multiple personality disorder, you mean," Victoria said.

"Yes. That might be possible, am I right?"

"Yes … but so far I haven't been able to find any indications for it in Diana's case. And really, Tim, it all sounds like something out of a lurid dime novel! I'm sure there's a far more harmless explanation. I am simply convinced of that."

A few more amorous words followed, then Tim and Victoria ended their phone call. She, however, was not yet ready to let the doctor's disappearance rest. Pearl and I now served as her interlocutors, and she continued to ponder it.

Of course Victoria didn't expect an answer from us; in fact, she didn't even know that we could understand her, but she probably preferred it to conducting a real soliloquy.

"Do you think Tim could be right?" she asked us. "Was Dr. Bachmann really murdered?"

"We mustn't rule it out, anyway," Pearl answered her—which, as I've said, she didn't understand.

"But who on earth could have had a reason to kill him?" Victoria continued. "Did he actually find out something during his examination of Juno that cost him his life? Does someone want the girl to stay sick when in truth there might be a cure for her? But who— her stepfather, who secretly detests her because she is not his flesh and blood? But he adores her, a blind man could see that! And Barbara is just as crazy about her, even though she seems to hate the rest of humanity. Her personality ... well, you've seen her for yourselves. Really quite a difficult old lady."

She began to cuddle Pearl, who had hopped up on the bed next to her.

Then she mused further: "Juno's lover—he appears to be crazy about her, but he seems almost too good to be true, don't you think?"

She earned an appreciative purr from Pearl. The midget really was pleased with our new assistant detective.

Next, the tutor was considered: "What about Chris Wieland? Is it possible that he just cannot stand his student anymore, and wants to get rid of her by slowly poisoning her and making it look like an incurable disease? And Dr. Bachmann was on his trail?"

She heaved a sigh. "What nonsense! Chris could just quit, couldn't he? It's not like he's a serf. Hmm, then we'd have that oddball old man, Thiele, who lives in the gatehouse. Maybe he hates children or teenagers? And maybe he knows all about the local poisonous plants?"

Pearl turned to me. "Do you remember that conversation in the library between Barbara and Chris? During the club meeting—remember she said to him that Daniel was after Juno's money? So Juno must be pretty rich. Victoria should know about that, I think."

"And how are you going to tell her?" I asked.

"Hmm, good question." Pearl wrinkled her nose in resignation. "I'm afraid I haven't the faintest idea."

"Maybe the doctor's murder—if he was murdered at all—wasn't about Juno," I objected. "That might be too obvious."

"Hmm. And what else could possibly be behind it?" Pearl enquired.

"Well, just as an example: in the TV crime shows, it's often the case that people who used to know each other earlier in life meet again by chance. People have a secret, and the other person knows it. And then a murder occurs."

"It happens quite often in the films with Poirot and Miss Marple," Pearl pronounced in the tones of a true connoisseur.

"Exactly. So could it be that when Dr. Bachmann came here to the castle, he recognized someone? A person he hadn't seen in many years—but whose secret he was now about to reveal?"

"Or Dr. Bachmann witnessed a crime," Pearl said, "here in the castle, and had to be eliminated. Witnesses live dangerously in almost every TV show, too, and some of them are stupid enough to try their hand at blackmail. Clearly, then, they have to be killed."

"But no crime has happened here in the castle," I said. "Or has it?"

Pearl growled in frustration. "Not that I know of."

"Maybe we just watch too many thrillers," I suggested. "Or rather, we've *experienced* too many thrillers. If the doctor really was killed, that would be the third murder we'll have had to solve. That can't be possible, can it?"

"Let's go to sleep, my little ones," Victoria cut into our conversation. "A little rest will certainly do us good."

12

But I was not yet ready to go to sleep. Apart from the matter of the missing doctor, there was something else that was giving me no peace: the ghost in the library.

I had as little experience with ghosts as I did with werewolves, and I certainly didn't want to make a fool of myself with a nameless fear. But then, I couldn't just forget my experiences in the library during the Wednesday Evening Club meeting. I had to get to the bottom of it, and find out the cause of the books falling on my head and the strange chill that had followed me.

I waited until Victoria and Pearl had fallen asleep, then I crept to the door, opened it as quietly as possible, and wandered down the stairs to the ground floor. The castle lay in complete darkness, and not a sound could be heard. The two-leggeds seemingly had all gone to sleep already—which was just fine by me.

Of course, if you're a dog you're not afraid of the dark, but I must confess that here in the castle, as I was walking through the nighttime corridors that seemed as gloomy as a tomb, I almost forgot that. There was something about the shadows that seemed to lurk behind the glass cases and statues and in the corners, something evil, it seemed to me, and something very much alive—not to mention hungry.

It was just as quiet and dark in the library when I entered it. Only a little moonlight fell into the room through the large glass panes.

Slowly I walked along the walls of shelves that stared down at me like lurking black giants. I kept sniffing, and watching carefully to see if I felt a cold draft, as I had during the club evening. I also glanced up every few steps to make sure the books were staying neat and tidy on their shelves instead of swooping down on me.

In this way I'd almost completed a whole round of the library—and already felt quite stupid, because I had believed in a ghost who threw books at me.

But—what can I say—at that very moment, a book literally jumped off its shelf and headed toward me. I just managed to get out of the line of fire with a daredevil leap, but I wasn't quite fast enough. The second book, which took off on its own, hit me on my back. I yelped involuntarily.

I would have loved to tuck in my tail and quickly seek the distance, but my pride forbade me to do so. I am a Malamute, a descendant of the fearless wolves of Alaska! My knees might have been trembling, I had to admit, but I was not so easily put to flight.

So I threw myself into an attack pose, stood wide-legged and bared my teeth in the direction of the bookshelf from whence I had been attacked.

Another book flew toward me. I now clearly saw that it didn't just fall off the shelf, but was pushed as if by an invisible hand.

The hairs on the back of my neck stood on end. I growled, snarled, and approached the shelf threateningly instead of fleeing. The smell of centuries-old animal skin—the leather covers of the old books—of dust and polish, laced with a bit of mustiness, rose to my nostrils.

And suddenly I saw it! The ghost—only for a brief moment she showed herself in front of me. A young girl, maybe twelve years old, in an old-fashioned dress. She appeared in front of the bookcase and hissed angrily at me—like Pearl when she was in a bad mood—but infinitely more frightening.

Before I could stop and fortify myself with further thoughts of my fearless ancestors, my paws took flight as if of their own accord. I heard a yelp that sounded like a puppy scared out of its wits, but I'm really embarrassed to admit that it must have come from my own throat. After all, I was the only dog to be seen.

I turned around and ran as fast as my paws would carry me toward the door, sliding and skidding on the parquet floor where there were no carpets, and when I reached the corridor I almost collided with Pearl.

She saved herself by jumping to the side before I could run head-on into her.

"Athos?" she cried in alarm. "What's the matter? What are you doing here? I woke up and you were gone."

My heart was beating like crazy. I had to pant for a while and get a grip on myself before I could answer Pearl's questions. I hoped fervently that she had not heard my frightened howling.

When I had gained back some self-control, I quickly

put on a heroic face and told her about the ghost in the library that had attacked me.

"A human girl, you say?" she commented after I'd finished. "And that scared you so much?"

"Who said anything about being scared?" I snapped back indignantly.

Was it just my imagination, or did the tiny one give me a pitying look? I really couldn't let her get away with that!

"See for yourself," I growled at her. "Go ahead—you're a cat; you're supposed to be endowed with psychic abilities, aren't you? At least, if Juno has her way."

Now she did seem reluctant after all. "You were probably just *hallunicating* that ghost girl," she said.

"For the last time it's called 'hallucinating'!" I retorted, somewhat unnerved. "But I certainly didn't imagine the books that fell on my head! Come on, what are you waiting for?" I goaded her. "See for yourself!"

At the same time, something in me wanted to keep her from putting herself in danger. She was so small, so defenseless...

Before I could stop her, she had already stomped into the library. Sure-footed and with her head held high—there she was, Pearl the Royal Tigress.

I stayed outside in the hallway, but peered after her, vowing to myself that I would save her if the book-throwing ghost attacked her as well.

She walked unmolested to the center of the room, stopped there and narrowed her eyes. I could just make out her expression in the moonlight. She stood there quite motionless, but I heard her meowing softly, calling for the ghost.

"Hello, young human? Are you there? Show yourself, I promise I won't hurt you."

Nothing moved on the shelves. Not a single book left the place where it belonged. But after a little while I felt as if I were seeing a shadow that was beginning to close in on Pearl. Again the hairs on the back of my neck stood up, and I felt as if I were being hit by another icy draft from the library.

Pearl also seemed to perceive something. She stretched her head towards the dusky phantom, then sat down on her hindquarters and continued meowing barely audibly.

It went on like this for quite a while until she finally stood up and returned to me.

"What was that all about?" I asked breathlessly. "Did you see something?"

"I think so," Pearl said. "But I'm not entirely sure. Maybe my psychic cat abilities aren't working properly—maybe I don't have any at all, because they don't form until you're a mature cat?"

"You *are* a mature cat," I said, "you just don't look it."

"Yeah, sure."

I'd never seen her so insecure.

"You can do anything an adult cat can do," I heard myself say. "Even a really big one. You're a fully-fledged tiger."

She licked with her tiny tongue over my snout. It tickled as if a beetle were cresting my nose.

Finally she reported hesitantly, "So either I'm imagining things, too, which would be no wonder in this house ... or there really is a ghost living in the library. A human girl? Oh, I really don't know, it was just a feeling—I couldn't see her, I just felt—how do you say it? A presence? It seemed to me that she wanted to talk to me. She said, 'You're such a cute little kitty. Watch out for the dog monster!'"

"The *dog monster*?" I repeated indignantly.

Pearl purred in conciliatory fashion. "Like I said, maybe I just imagined it all."

"Dog monster ... pah!"

13

The next morning, Victoria continued to snoop—much to Pearl's delight. The doctor's sudden disappearance seemed to give her no peace.

Immediately after breakfast, she said, "Let's go for a walk, little ones," which we immediately recognized as an excuse. She was not in the mood for exercise; she was looking for answers. But of course we were to go along for the ride.

Victoria actually took us for a short walk through the castle park, but all too soon she headed purposely for the narrow ridge that lay between the building and the river gorge. She came to stand right under Diana's balcony—that is, at the spot where Diana had said she had seen the doctor's body.

The area here, as I've already mentioned, was somewhat wider and covered with gravel, and directly on the cliff edge some low bushes grew that formed a natural barrier to the abyss. One would not fall unintentionally into the depths here. However, if one wanted to throw someone down one could squeeze through between the bushes with the body without any problems, and let the unpleasant ballast disappear into the ravine, never to be seen again.

But that in turn meant that any corpse lying under Diana's balcony would never have rolled into the depths under its own power.

Victoria knelt down on the gravel surface, but there were no visible traces of a person lying here last night. There was no blood to be seen; besides, it had rained in the early morning hours.

My dog's nose, however, picked up a scent. I walked in circles several times, my muzzle close to the gravel, and finally said to Pearl with conviction: "He was lying here, I'm sure of it." I even thought I smelled blood, very faintly, but I wouldn't have put my paw in the fire for that.

Pearl did some sniffing of her own, but her cat nose was no match for mine. We dogs are simply better in this area.

"The smell of the doctor?" she asked me. "Are you sure?"

"Not completely," I had to admit. After all, I had hardly known Dr. Bachmann, and had only caught his scent in my nose once or twice. But if my memory did not deceive me, it smelled like him here on the gravel surface.

There were other smells in the immediate vicinity, belonging to various occupants of the house: I thought I detected Bastian's smoky aroma, as well as Sendrik's far more pleasant scent, and Barbara's flowery smell.

But when I pointed this out to Pearl, she just said, "Maybe they've already looked around here also, after Diana's claims last night? Or maybe they came by in the last few days—on a walk, which may have been quite harmless. After all, there's a great view from here."

"True," I had to concede. "But the doctor was lying here on the gravel," I repeated, after sniffing the area in question again. "And he certainly didn't do it for fun."

"So he *was* murdered, I should think," Pearl opined.

"I wouldn't go that far right now. He could have—I don't know—fallen off one of the terraces. An accident ... or maybe he even tried to commit suicide?"

"Then why would anyone have made his body disappear?" Pearl objected.

"Hmm," I grumbled, because I really didn't know the answer to her question.

"Murders always seem to happen around us," Pearl continued to argue. "Haven't you noticed that yet? So the doctor must have been killed."

Cat logic; I made no reply. I didn't like the idea one bit.

"What if the doctor wasn't dead yet," I suggested, "and for whatever reason he ended up here. Let's say he was able to get up again, drag himself a little way, but was so disoriented that he fell into the abyss."

"Possibly," Pearl said, but she didn't look very convinced.

I walked along the bushes that lined the precipice. At one point it smelled of the doctor—at least I had that impression—but only fleetingly. Moreover, the scent was again overlaid by numerous others. Only a trained and very experienced police dog would have been able to tell who exactly had been in which place and, above all, when.

If things went on like this, with Pearl and me and the constant stream of bodies, maybe I should take a course for sniffer dogs. But how could I ever explain that to Victoria?

I squeezed my way between two lath-like plants and stared into the gorge. The waterfall was rushing and rumbling, and I got a fine spray from it, which the wind drove toward me.

I turned to Pearl: "We need to search the ravine for the doctor. If he didn't go straight down the waterfall and land in that little pool down there, his body must have gotten caught somewhere among the trees and rocks on the slope here below us."

"You want to go down *there*?" Pearl exclaimed, her eyes wide. "We're not mountain goats!"

Pearl was more of a sofa cat; daredevil adventures in the wild were not her thing.

At that moment, Victoria, who had been concentrating on the gravel area under Diana's balcony, spied me.

"Athos!" she cried, startled. "Stay away from there! It's dangerous!"

I heard the alarm in her voice and ran back to her.

Diagonally above our heads a terrace door opened. Sendrik immediately leaned over the railing and spotted us. "Ah, good morning, Victoria. What are you up to?"

Apparently, her loud call to me had caught his attention.

"Wait," he said before she could answer, "I'll join you down there."

Less than two minutes later he rounded the back corner of the castle and headed over toward us.

"You're investigating the area here, I see?" he concluded with sound logic. "I already did that this morning with Bastian. Were you able to find anything?"

Victoria tilted her head and looked down at me. "I can't detect anything peculiar, but my dog seems to have scented something." She shrugged.

Once again I cursed the impossibility of clear communication between us. I could have told her that Dr. Bachmann had almost certainly been lying here, and that perhaps one of the castle residents had carried him the short distance to the precipice. He had not been dragged; otherwise one would certainly have been able to make out traces of it in the gravel.

On the other hand, the murderer—if he existed—could have removed such telltale traces entirely at his leisure during the night. Smoothing the gravel again would not have been a difficult task.

And in the end you didn't have to be a muscleman to be able to carry Dr. Bachmann for a few steps. He had been pretty small for a two-legged.

"If Diana really saw Dr. Bachmann's body down here," Victoria told Sendrik, "he must have disappeared almost immediately afterwards. A few minutes later we were already with her—and he was gone."

Sendrik nodded, lost in thought. "I don't know what to wish for more," he said, after a small moment of silence. "That Diana is not delusional and actually saw something..."

He shook his head. "No; that would mean that some-thing really has happened to our doctor."

"Yes, the idea is horrible," Victoria said. "But I hon-estly can't imagine him packing his things in the mid-dle of the night and leaving the house without saying a word—apart from that note to Barbara. And that could have been written by God-knows-who..."

Sendrik nodded. Then he suddenly looked around furtively, as if to make sure he was alone with Victoria.

He lowered his voice and said, "You know, it's possi-ble that Barbara actually made up this alleged mes-sage."

"Excuse me?"

"What I'm saying is—I can think of a reason why Dr. Bachmann might have run away. You see, I had a con-versation with him yesterday morning, and I accused him of being hired by Barbara in order to keep Juno from marrying Daniel. She has already received a pro-posal from him ... I told you that, didn't I? She hasn't accepted yet, to my knowledge, but I think it's only a matter of time. She's crazy about the guy." He bared his teeth in a tentative smile.

"And Barbara objects to that connection," Victoria said. "You've mentioned that before, too."

"Oh yeah, she hates Daniel. No one is good enough for her little Juno. She wants to shield the girl from everything and everyone, and would prefer to lock her in the highest tower of the castle. So I suspected that Dr. Bachmann—on Barbara's behalf—would come to the conclusion during his examination that Juno is really terribly ill. Incurable, with gloomy prospects for the future, that sort of thing. To scare Daniel off with his diagnosis, you see. I approached Dr. Bachmann about it yesterday, accused him outright—and he buckled."

"Unbelievable," Victoria said. "I really wouldn't have thought Barbara capable of that. And you're saying that Dr. Bachmann went along with it?"

Sendrik scowled. "Unfortunately, Barbara will stop at nothing when it comes to getting her way. As far as Dr. Bachmann is concerned, you're right; it surprised me too. But to get back to his disappearance—I could well imagine that he went on the run after I unmasked his true mission. And as I said, Barbara could have made up the goodbye message easily. It would be understandable if he didn't want to continue with the set-up after I had seen through him, no matter what sum Barbara had offered him. Dr. Bachmann may still be young, and not entirely averse to money, but believe it or not most people who become doctors have a high moral code. They really want to help, and making a wrong diagnosis ... that's anything but a peccadillo."

Sendrik broke off and stared down at the tips of his shoes. When he raised his head again, he looked exhausted.

"Forgive me," he said to Victoria. "I really didn't want to burden you with our family problems."

"Not at all, that's perfectly all right," she demurred. "I came here to help Diana, after all. And that includes her family," she added.

Sendrik smiled wanly. "That's really kind of you. I always thought of myself as quite resilient, equipped with a robust nervous system. But it's all getting to be too much for me. Juno's health, and now Diana's, um, episodes—Barbara the dragon—my brother stalking my wife…"

Victoria raised her eyebrows in amazement.

His smile widened, albeit in melancholy fashion. "You wonder how I know that? It's hard to miss, isn't it? And Bastian and I have never been the best of friends. He only lives in our house because of Diana; I should throw him out, but then I can't bring myself to do that."

Victoria murmured a few words of astonishment, then tried to comfort Sendrik. After that, the two of them started moving. They turned to the right, probably to take a little walk through the castle park while they were talking to each other.

The opportunity seemed favorable.

"You stay with Victoria," I said to Pearl. "If anything happens, sound the alarm, alright? I'll be around."

"'Around'? Where do you mean to go?"

I turned my head toward the abyss. "I told you before—we have to make sure that Dr. Bachmann is really dead. I'll search this slope for him."

Pearl looked at me as if I had lost my mind.

"It'll be fine," I said. "I'm good at climbing."

That was a lie. Or, rather, I had no idea how good I was at climbing. I hadn't had too many opportunities in my life so far to find out.

But at least I had two legs more than any human being, and if those chamois with their impractical hooves could clamber around on the bare rocky slopes as if they were just going for a walk, I could probably manage to climb down a wooded slope with my five-clawed paws. How to get back up ... well, I'd think about how to do that later.

I started down before Pearl could protest, and soon I had climbed the first twenty or thirty meters into the depths. Or should I say slithered? Fortunately the slope was wooded, so that every now and then a saving bush or tree trunk stood in my way and slowed my descent.

I don't want to go into detail here about one or another terrifying moment I experienced, otherwise I'll end up looking like a scaredy-cat.

Let us say only two things. First: a Malamute is definitely not equal to a chamois in steep terrain. And second: I eventually did find Dr. Bachmann. And he was dead as a doornail.

14

The way back was surprisingly easier than the descent had been. It hadn't helped to stare into the abyss at every step and thus look death in the eye. Uphill I was spared that.

I was careful where I put my paws, and my claws gave me a passable grip. It seemed to take me half an eternity, and I had to traverse the slope several times in a zigzag pattern to avoid the steepest parts, but eventually I reached the top and with it the castle park.

Victoria and Pearl had left the place under Diana's balcony. However I could hear my human's voice, which seemed to be coming from the castle's main driveway.

I walked in that direction, until Victoria appeared in my field of vision. She was standing next to the road in front of the gatehouse that guarded the entrance to the estate, and was engaged in conversation with Thiele, the oddball old man and former friend of the late master of the establishment.

Pearl was lying a little way apart on a flat stone and sunbathing. She could have been mistaken for a furry lizard or some reptile that depended on the warmth of the sun to keep its body temperature from dropping too low. But cats are definitely not cold-blooded animals, as strange as Pearl might be in some other respects.

When she saw me, she looked relieved. Her gaze roamed over my fur, which had definitely been messed up quite a bit by the climb. The next moment she stretched out on her rock, then hopped down and ran towards me.

"Lie down," she ordered, "you look terrible."

I did as I was told, and Pearl set about cleaning my fur. She was also kind enough to pull a thorn out of my nose, which had become painfully stuck in there.

"I found him," I reported before Pearl could ask me about Dr. Bachmann. "He's dead."

"Murdered?" Pearl asked eagerly—only to add in an expert tone, "Gunshot injuries? Puncture wounds? Signs of poisoning?"

"Just a crushed skull and lots of broken bones," I said. "He definitely fell. Whether he had an accident, jumped voluntarily or was pushed, though, I can't say. There's a bloody wound on the back of his head that might have stemmed from a blow."

"He could have gotten it in his fall, too," Pearl said.

"Yeah, that's right. Both explanations are possible, I suppose." I wasn't an expert like those forensic doctors in our TV crime shows, who knew how to derive the most amazing insights just from wounds and injuries. Sometimes they could read half a victim's life story from his corpse—and at the same time find out *who* had killed the person. In that respect, the two-leggeds were quite clever.

"But there was something else," I said to Pearl. "Dr. Bachmann was still wearing the jacket he wore to the club meeting that night; dark blue with gold buttons. And one of them was missing."

"The one we found in Diana's room?" said Pearl.

"I think so. The buttons on the jacket looked the same, anyway. Oh, and I spotted Dr. Bachmann's luggage, too—a big brown leather suitcase. The thing either crashed down along with the doctor or was thrown into the abyss after him. It lay no more than thirty meters from the body, a little higher up the slope, where it was caught among some trees. The lock had cracked open, and there were men's clothes in the suitcase that smelled like the doctor. So it must have been his luggage."

"Then he *was* murdered," Pearl insisted. "Surely he wasn't going to voluntarily leave the castle by climbing down the escarpment, dragging his suitcase with him. Not even a human is *that* crazy. And if he'd wanted to kill himself, he certainly wouldn't have taken the luggage with him. There is definitely something wrong with this death, Athos! The murderer made the suitcase disappear on purpose, I tell you, so that the story of the doctor's sudden departure would be believable. We must lead our assistant detective to the body!"

She glanced at Victoria, who was still talking animatedly with old Thiele.

"We will do nothing of the sort," I protested. "The body is in very rough terrain. We can't take a two-legged there without running the risk of breaking their neck!"

"Okay, okay ... but Victoria has to know that Dr.

Bachmann is dead! How else are we supposed to fill her in?"

I didn't have an answer to her question, as usual when it came to communicating something to our human—or any other two-legged for that matter. It was so annoying.

Pearl and I both fell silent, and therefore I could eavesdrop on the conversation between Victoria and old Thiele.

"I hear and see things here in the castle and on the grounds, you know," he'd just announced in an ominous tone, raising his eyebrows. "At my age you don't sleep so well, and then you just wander around like an old castle ghost."

"And what *did* you hear or see?" asked Victoria. Her tone sounded a little impatient, not to say annoyed. Regrettably I had missed out on their conversation so far, so I had no way of knowing what the old man had already revealed to our assistant detective. Or maybe he hadn't—was he merely dropping vague hints?

"There's something you should know," said Thiele. "Young Juno is not half as innocent and naive as she would lead us to believe. She's got it all figured out, I tell you! Alexander, her late father—God rest his soul!—she had him wrapped around her little finger! She always got what she wanted, no matter how crazy her wishes were."

Victoria now seemed more interested, more attentive, but said nothing that might interrupt the old man's flow of speech.

His voice swelled; the subject seemed to upset him greatly. "You should have seen the massive quantities of toys Alexander bought her when she was little. Tons of unnecessary stuff! Even then the brat had a firm grip on him. And as a child she already had three rooms, a suite fit for a king's daughter, furnished by some spiv who called himself an interior designer! Alexander also bought her designer clothes and shoes, jewelry, and God knows what else."

Thiele waved his bony hands in Victoria's face. "But God punishes the greedy, the ones who are never satisfied! That's why the girl is wasting away now, I tell you. She's only gotten what she deserved."

His eyes narrowed, abruptly reminding me of a bird of prey.

Brim-full of disgust, he added: "That is, if the supposed illness of our dear Juno is not also just theater. Another means to an end, so that she can get everything she wants—from Barbara, now. She is just as crazy about her. *Poor little Juno!*" he mimicked Barbara's voice.

"What an odd idea," Victoria said. "You can't miss Juno's poor health, even if you're not a medical professional. She's certainly not faking that."

"How would you know? You're not a doctor, are you? Just a shrink—no offense," the old man added and forced himself to smile wryly.

Victoria could find nothing to say in reply.

"Don't you think it's strange that this Dr. Bachmann has suddenly run away?" Thiele asked suddenly. "Who knows what he found out about poor, sick Juno! And whether he wasn't deliberately removed because of it ... do you understand me?"

Victoria frowned.

"I find his disappearance strange, too," she relented finally. "But to get back to Juno: I really think you're misjudging her. Mr. Messner may well have spoiled her too much during his lifetime—that's what people do, and usually only with the best intentions. He loved his daughter very much, and perhaps did her no favors from a pedagogical point of view by fulfilling her every wish. But that she manipulated him in the way you describe? I really can't imagine that; Juno seems to me to be a friendly and very kind young lady."

"Ha!" the old man grinned. "Then I guess she's got you wrapped around her finger, too! Just like the others. Didn't I tell you she's a master at it, that little snake? Her friendliness, her whole innocent poor-girl act is pure facade, I tell you. Pure calculation!"

He kicked at a rock lying on the side of the road with his shoe and watched it skip away.

Then he turned to Victoria once again. "An irony of fate, I say, that she is now being ripped off in her turn by that good-for-nothing Kirsch. A gold-digger and a womanizer, that's what he is! He'll break the brat's heart, and then she'll finally get what she deserves."

15

Late that afternoon, just before dinner, Pearl and I witnessed an interesting phone conversation that cast Daniel Kirsch in a new light.

We had taken a siesta in the castle park, the sun blazing down upon us again, while Victoria had stayed indoors.

Daniel drove up in one of those vehicles that humans call vintage cars. Usually, our dear two-legged friends like to throw old things away instead of repairing them or giving them to others, but when it comes to old cars it's a different story. It seems that the older the car, the more valuable it is.

Anyway, Daniel had driven up in just such a vehicle. It was silver-colored, very sleek, and emblazoned on the hood was a leaping predatory cat ornament. A Jaguar, as Pearl—expert on cats of all kinds—assured me. She was of the opinion that Victoria should also drive such a car.

As Daniel got out of the vehicle, his cell phone rang. He took it out of his pocket, glanced at the display and stopped. Instead of walking toward the house, he turned instead and strolled away from the castle and into the park.

"Come on, after him," Pearl said, suddenly chipper. "We've got to hear what he's saying. I think he has something to hide."

No sooner said than done; once again we were the irreproachable pets who just wanted to stretch our paws a bit, and so we followed Juno's boyfriend. He did notice us, but didn't pay us any attention or even feel pursued.

He seemed uncomfortable with the phone call he was receiving. He furrowed his brow and spoke in a pressed voice: "You'll have to be patient a little longer—I'll pay up. I really don't understand why you can't defer an installment or two for me—"

I couldn't hear the answer of the person he was talking to; perhaps the man was speaking very quietly, or Daniel's cell phone was a model that was not as sound-permeable on the outside as some others were.

Anyway, the answer Daniel received didn't seem to please him one bit.

"You really are cutthroats!" he hissed into the phone. "I'll soon be a rich man, count on it, and I'll pay it all back at once and find a more reputable institution!"

He hung up angrily.

"Oh, dear me," Pearl meowed. "I suppose he's in desperate need of money—do you think he's really just taking advantage of Juno like that Thiele guy claimed?"

"It could be worse," I said. "Possibly that's why he wants to marry her so quickly, so he can inherit her money," I said, putting into words the thought that had popped into my head during Daniel's phone call. "She's supposed to be rich, isn't she? And very sick."

"Where's he going now?" Pearl exclaimed.

Daniel had put his phone back in his pocket and was

now walking towards the castle.

We just managed to slip into the house behind him before the heavy front door slammed shut with a bang.

In the hall he ran right into Barbara.

"You again," she hissed like a real dragon when she caught sight of him. "Don't you have a job to go to instead of hanging around here with us all the time?" I was a little surprised that Daniel wasn't hit by flames from her mouth.

However, he was not intimidated.

"You'd better get used to me," he returned in an equally unfriendly tone. "I'll be Juno's husband soon enough, whether you like it or not." Then he simply left the elderly woman standing there and hurried straight into the library.

When he opened the door Pearl ran between his legs and purred at him, which meant something like, "Come on, human, pick me up and take me with you."

Who'd be surprised that Daniel did as he was told, even though he couldn't understand Pearl's words? He bent down, took her in his arms and then entered the library with her—where Juno was already waiting for him.

I slipped into the room behind them, walking on my own four paws. No one ever thought of picking *me* up and carrying me around. Life really was unfair.

The library seemed to be one of Juno's favorite places in the castle. She was sitting on a sofa, her legs stretched out in front of her under a blanket, with some thick pillows at her back. When she saw Daniel, she smiled, lowered the book she had just been reading, and held out her arms to him. Then she spotted Pearl and let out the usual cry of delight.

Daniel got a passionate kiss, while Pearl was allowed to make herself comfortable on Juno's lap. Meanwhile Daniel took a seat on the edge of the sofa.

"She's so cute," Juno chirped as she petted Pearl. "Do you think we could have a cat, too? And maybe a dog—but a smaller one than Athos. Do you think Barbara would allow it?"

Daniel's smile died. "Always Barbara," he cried, seized by sudden anger. "She's such a bully! You've got to stop letting her boss you around, dear!"

Juno smiled uncertainly. Then she averted her eyes from her lover and petted Pearl with renewed abandon—while I wondered why anyone would want a smaller dog than me.

Daniel wasn't done yet, however. "Juno, how many times do I have to ask you? You do love me, don't you? Let's get married and get out of here, so that no one can boss you around at last."

"But—" she began, but he wouldn't let her get a word in edgewise.

"Dr. Bachmann disappearing so suddenly ... don't you think that means something?" he asked with a somber look.

Now Juno's smile disappeared as well. She was not very strong, but she struggled to sit up on the sofa.

"And what is that supposed to mean?" she returned defiantly. "That I'm incurable, and that's why he ran away? Because he doesn't want me as a patient anymore?"

"What? No, where did you get that idea?" Daniel demanded in surprise. "Don't you think—"

He paused abruptly, seeming to debate with himself about how to proceed, or even whether this conversation was a good idea.

"Don't you think someone here in the house means you harm?" he finally said with new determination. He grabbed Juno's hand.

I approached the two of them in order to settle down next to the sofa, from where I would have them both in view—and in front of my nose. Humans, just like us four-leggeds, also communicate with each other via their body odors, even if they usually don't notice it consciously.

Juno and Daniel both smelled very excited now, and he quite angry at that.

But at that moment I saw it: the ghost!

It—or rather she, namely the young girl I had briefly spied the previous night—appeared in front of the sofa, pushed herself between Juno and me, and waved her arms like crazy.

A yelp escaped me, and I must report to my shame that I almost fell off my paws from sheer fright.

The ghost, however, seemed equally frightened. The girl contorted her face, backed away from me, and the next moment she was gone.

Pearl jumped excitedly from Juno's lap and stared after the apparition. So she had seen her, too.

Immediately afterwards, the image of the ghostly girl flared up once again, this time behind the sofa. She appeared to me to be just like a mist, which was condensing and dissolving again at the same time.

Pearl showed amazing courage.

"Hello," she called to the apparition, meowing. "Who are you? What's your name?"

She did not receive an answer.

Apparently dead two-leggeds—if that really was the nature of this phenomenon—could not understand our language any more than the living representatives of the species did.

But I was wrong about that.

Pearl continued the conversation unabashedly, much as if she were having a chat with me.

"Do you have something against Athos?" she asked the phantasm, who now remained motionless behind the sofa. "He's quite tame, you know. You don't have to be afraid of him."

I didn't like to hear that—who wants to be called 'quite tame'? But to my great astonishment the ghost actually gave Pearl an answer this time. So the dead girl understood us after all!

"He's a *dog*," she told Pearl in disgust. "And dogs are evil. They bite!"

The words did not come out of her mouth, although her lips were moving. Rather they seemed to form directly in my head, in much the same way as was often the case in conversations with other animals. My heart almost stopped with shock.

"Look, Daniel," Juno exclaimed enthusiastically, "I think they can see our castle ghost again! They're talking to her!"

She turned her head jerkily, staring at the spot behind the sofa that Pearl and I were focusing on, but couldn't seem to see anything of the ghost girl herself.

"Please don't change the subject," Daniel said in a serious tone. He seemed completely indifferent to the spirit.

Juno was not deterred, however. "I believe I can sense her, even if I don't see her. She's sad, I think; lonely. Yet she loves this library as much as I do. Don't you?" She shouted the last words into the room, looking around again as if she didn't know which way to turn.

"Juno, I beg you, stop this humbug!" Daniel cried. He grabbed both of her hands and leaned close over her. "Look at me, please. I really think you might be in danger. I don't like it at all that Dr. Bachmann just disappeared like that."

"Oh, what nonsense! Who would want to do me harm? And why?"

The ghost behind the sofa vanished into thin air and did not return even after Pearl called out to it several times.

I now turned my full attention to the conversation that was unfolding between Daniel and Juno.

"You're so naive, my dear!" exclaimed Daniel. "That's delightful on the one hand ... but also dangerous on the other! Because of your millions, of course! Barbara is against me and against our marriage because she wants to continue managing your fortune. And I'm pretty sure she would climb over several dead bodies for that. Even over yours, my darling!"

She tried to pull her hands away from him, but he held them tightly.

"Don't look at me like that," he cried, "I'm just worried about you! And who knows how conscientiously Barbara manages your money. I wonder if she hasn't long since been tempted to divert some of the funds for her own benefit. You could ask to see her records, to keep an eye on her, don't you think? You're old enough for that."

Juno shook her head. "I trust her. Granted, she's very strict, but she means well, I'm sure of it."

Daniel wasn't ready to give up yet. "What if she brought this doctor into the house to hurt you? Blast it, do we even know if he really was a doctor at all? Maybe he got cold feet and she had to ... get rid of him."

"You're crazy!" shouted Juno.

He finally let go of her, raising his hands to placate her.

"Anyway, dear, I beg you: let us leave here together. Let's have no one sabotage our love anymore. And we'll find you a really fantastic doctor. There just has to be someone who can help you, I'm firmly convinced of that!"

"My stepfather *is* a good doctor," Juno protested. "He's really trying hard with me. Besides, I can't just leave here. Mom needs me, after all—I can't abandon her."

"She has a massive alcohol problem, dear, can't you see that?"

"That may be so, but that's even more reason why I mustn't leave her."

The two debated back and forth for a while, but when the gong calling them for dinner finally sounded, Daniel gave up. He helped Juno off the sofa and supported her on the way out of the library.

Pearl and I followed closely behind them. I looked forward to dinner with great pleasure; not the one to be eaten by the two-leggeds in the large castle dining room, but that which hopefully awaited Pearl and me downstairs with Francesco, the friendly cook.

"So Juno is loaded," Pearl exclaimed excitedly as we trotted toward the kitchen. "She must have inherited her father's fortune. And Barbara manages it. Did I get that right?"

"I think so," I said.

"Victoria needs to know about that. It's important!" the tiny one enthused.

I did not have to tell her what was obvious: that again, there was no possibility for us to give this new-found knowledge to our two-legged friend.

16

The next morning Juno consulted with her tutor over her love for Daniel. Apparently Mr. Wieland not only taught her various subjects, but was also the girl's close confidant.

I can't claim that I was systematically shadowing Juno; I'd come to overhear the conversation for quite different reasons. I had followed Juno this morning into the small writing room, in which the instruction took place, out of quite egocentric motives. As has probably become clear by now I am an education-hungry dog, and so I wanted to hear what Chris was teaching his student. I was wondering if I could learn something new from him, too.

Unfortunately, getting Victoria to hire me a tutor would be an almost hopeless endeavor—I was under no illusions about that.

Pearl had preferred to devote herself to her beauty sleep that morning, and Victoria was also still in bed when I'd left for class and positioned myself in front of Juno's sofa in the study room. She was half-lying there in a comfortable position, presumably because sitting on a chair for long periods of time would have taken too much of her strength.

Without wanting to, I had to think of the words of old Thiele: that Juno was in fact in perfect health and was only faking her illness.

Looking at her, I found it hard to believe. Just lying around, even breathing, seemed difficult for her on some days.

Before Chris Wieland could begin his lesson today, Juno had asked him for advice about Daniel's marriage proposal. She told him about the conversation I'd witnessed the previous day—very truthfully, if my memory did not deceive me.

When she'd finished, she added, "You always have such sensible ideas, Mr. Wieland. What would you advise me to do?"

He took quite a while before giving her an answer, and his words came hesitantly.

"It's really none of my business, Juno, but since you asked, um ... you do realize that Daniel doesn't have a very good reputation, right?"

Juno's brow furrowed. "Well, yes ... he used to be ... oh, I don't want to dig into the past. People can change, you know!"

Mr. Wieland nodded soberly. Then he said, "But there's no hurry, is there? Why not wait until you are eighteen for the wedding? If he really loves you, he won't rush you. And then we can continue your lessons. That's important to you too, isn't it?"

He approached her and lovingly patted her head. I looked up at him and sniffed him as he did so, but I could not tell whether this was merely the tender gesture of a teacher, who had known his student for a long time and had taken her into his heart, or if Chris Wieland was approaching Juno as a man who wanted her for himself—instead of leaving her to someone else, much older, of whom he didn't have a particularly good opinion to boot? Was his advice in the end merely due to jealousy?

Chris was a very quiet guy, one who didn't show his true feelings and had a very good grip on himself, even confusing my otherwise quite-passable nose with his restraint. And he certainly would have made a more suitable husband for Juno. Not only was he considerably younger than Daniel, but he seemed to me to be a quiet, reliable, and very learned person.

"You're a good teacher," Juno said—which didn't sound much like a declaration of love.

Chris acknowledged the compliment with a thin smile, then withdrew his hand, which had been resting on Juno's shoulder.

"I'd ask you not to tell Daniel about this conversation," he said at last. "He mustn't know what I think of him, because if you do end up marrying him I don't wish to turn him against me. I want to keep teaching you, Juno, because I know you have great potential. Maybe you would like to study at university later on— via distance learning, and I could support you. Would you like that?"

Juno's eyes lit up. "Sure! I'd like to study literature and then specialize in Gothic novels. Or psychology like Victoria, that would be exciting too. Would both be possible?"

"It would take a lot of work, but you're hardworking and smart, so you'd be able to succeed," Mr. Wieland said.

"If I marry Daniel, then Barbara would have to give me my money, even if I am only sixteen. Otherwise I won't get it till I'm eighteen."

Chris nodded. This information didn't seem new to him. But from the look on his face, he didn't consider this possible gain in freedom a valid reason to marry Daniel.

"We could take a trip around the world, all of us together," Juno continued. Her voice sounded bright as a bell, and some color had come into her pale face. The subject seemed to excite her.

"On a ship," she added. "I could rest there when I'm not feeling well and still see the world. That would be perfect. And wouldn't you enjoy a trip like that?"

"I certainly would, but still ... I'd really wait a bit before getting married if I were you, Juno."

She ignored his objection. "I think Mom and Sendrik would be very happy, too, if Barbara would stop bossing them around. She's really very strict, isn't she...?"

17

Over the course of the day, Juno's condition deteriorated. In the evening she was feeling so bad that she decided to just have dinner in bed instead of joining the others in the castle's dining room that night.

Daniel came to visit Juno after work, as he so often did, just before dinner. But she wanted to see even him only briefly today.

She complained of pain, nausea, *the full rigmarole*, as she put it.

It seemed to me that she bore her illness and her failing health in general very bravely, but sometimes—as today—she fell into a depressed mood in which everything seemed gloomy and hopeless to her.

"Have dinner with us anyway," Diana told Daniel, and he accepted the invitation.

He must have regretted it by the time the appetizers were being served, because the atmosphere in the dining room that evening can only be described as harrowing. There was little conversation, Barbara was shooting Daniel hostile looks, and even Sendrik, who had been trying hard to start a polite conversation, soon threw in the towel.

Therefore I wasn't surprised to see Daniel leave right after the main course had been served, claiming fatigue and a lack of appetite. Besides, there was supposedly still a lot of work waiting for him at home.

"I'll check on Juno for a minute and come back tomorrow," he explained before leaving the room.

After dessert came at last, officially ending the dinner, Barbara rose from her seat. It seemed to me that she had little interest in staying in the family circle if Juno wasn't present.

Sendrik excused himself a few minutes later, and Chris Wieland also left immediately after him. Victoria remained seated; she had started a conversation with Bastian about wines. This was not a topic that interested me, and so I did not follow their interaction any further.

When the remaining two-leggeds had finally moved on to coffee and spirits, Pearl and I decided it was high time for our own dinner—that is, not the dry food Victoria was still regularly providing for us, but a visit to Francesco in the castle kitchen.

To be exact, I entered the kitchen while Pearl waited outside in the hallway with a hungry look on her face. After all, we preferred that Francesco should not suffer an allergic attack, but rather spoil us with his cooking skills.

I managed to get a few tasty morsels for both of us from the friendly cook, which the midget and I ate right away in the corridor.

Thereupon we allowed ourselves a little nap. Our days in the castle had really been anything but a relaxing vacation, and even a four-pawed detective had to take a break now and then.

As far as the deceased—presumably murdered—Dr.

Bachmann was concerned, we had not yet made any progress. The people in the castle had come to terms with the explanation of his hasty departure, despite showing some doubts. In any case, they were not looking for him, and Pearl and I hadn't yet found a way to tell them about the body in the ravine. In short we were a little stumped in our role as detectives, a fact that neither Pearl nor I liked one bit.

After we'd rested for a little while, Pearl woke me up with a dampening face wash and then suggested we visit Juno. In her opinion, cat cuddling was the cure-all remedy par excellence for two-leggeds, and she wanted to selflessly make herself available to Juno in this regard so that the girl would feel better again.

Our visit would cheer Juno up anyway, I thought, so the tiny one and I walked up the stairs to the second floor where her rooms were located.

But no sooner had we climbed the last of the steps than Chris Wieland came rushing toward us in the corridor above. There was an expression of fear on his face—or was it disgust?

He ran past us so fast that I couldn't really see. It wouldn't have taken much for him to step on Pearl, so I growled at him. As a two-legged, you ought to watch your step when a tiny cat was under the same roof. My protest, however, passed him by unnoticed. He just ran along the corridor and in the next moment had already disappeared around a corner.

"What's wrong with him?" Pearl asked, startled. "Has he seen a ghost?"

She arched her back, complaining after the fact about her near miss with disaster, and then sniffed left and right as if to use her newfound paranormal sleuthing skills.

But if there was indeed a ghost here in the corridor, Pearl could not detect it. Which was just fine with me; one ghost in the library was quite enough.

We ran after the teacher but he only disappeared into his room, which was situated further back in the corridor, and the door slammed shut behind him.

Pearl and I sat there perplexed for a moment, wondering if he would return, and if we might overhear some conversation in which he explained himself to another two-legged—but he didn't do us that favor.

So we went to see Juno as we had planned. Her stepfather was just leaving the room and was very surprised to see us.

"Don't tell me you two are paying Juno a visit?" he said. "I'm sure she'd love that! Except she's already asleep, unfortunately."

We peered into the room through the open door and found that he was right, so we left without having achieved anything.

We spent the rest of the evening in Victoria's bedroom. Our human made another phone call to Tim and then afterwards read a mystery novel—for which she earned purring praise from Pearl, but only because there was no TV in the guest suite. Finally, once it was quite late, Victoria went to sleep.

Personally, I wouldn't have minded a quiet, uneventful night myself—but once again my wish wasn't granted.

18

Almost at the stroke of midnight, a noise jolted me from sleep.

I sat up straight, inadvertently giving Pearl a rather rude shove. She had once again been sleeping on my front paw.

"Hey!" she protested sleepily. "What are you doing?"

I quickly mumbled an apology, then listened into the darkness.

Screams!—I hadn't been mistaken—followed by sobs, as if someone were crying their eyes out. The sounds were muffled by the walls of the castle, but they were clearly coming from the direction of Diana's room. Again? Had she made another gruesome discovery?

Victoria continued to slumber peacefully while I was already walking towards the door.

"Come on, hurry, Diana needs help!" I called out to the kitten, making a beeline for the door handle, and the next moment Pearl and I were galloping down the hall.

The screams, which by now had turned into panicked howls, were indeed coming from Diana's room. I stood on my hind paws, trying to push down her door handle, but this time I was out of luck. The door was locked.

I was about to run back to our room to alert Victoria,

but Pearl stopped me. "Wait, and be quiet! Can't you hear it? Someone's coming."

I looked around the corridor.

"No," Pearl said, "inside the room. That was the door to the next room that just opened there. And now the footsteps are leading ... into Diana's bedroom."

She was right. Now I noticed the sounds too—and in the next moment I heard a voice I recognized. It belonged to Sendrik; apparently, his wife's wailing had awakened him, and he'd run into her bedroom.

"Diana?" he cried. "What's the matter, darling?"

The next instant a scream escaped *him.*

Then I could hear his voice again. It sounded agitated, no—scared to death. "My God, Diana, what happened? What have you done?"

Pearl and I pressed ourselves against the wood of the door to be able to hear better.

"I ... I don't know," Diana stammered. "He ... attacked me, I think. Knocked me unconscious. Is he ... dead?" Her voice broke.

"You *think*?" her husband replied, stunned.

"Sendrik found a dead body?" I concluded. "In there, in Diana's bedroom?"

Pearl's nose was twitching so excitedly it was almost vibrating. "Sounds like it," she replied, "but *who* is it?"

Neither Sendrik nor Diana told us that.

Silence fell within the room for a brief moment, then Sendrik said, "Yes, he's dead. I can't do anything for him." His voice sounded changed; breathless and subdued. He seemed to be having a hard time not to lose his head completely.

Another pause arose, then he asked his wife, "He attacked you, you say?" His words were full of skepticism, a reproach that couldn't be ignored resonating in his tone.

No wonder, then, that Diana felt attacked. "Yes! I told you so," she defended herself. "I ... merely tried to fight him off, I'm sure of it! I would never—"

Sendrik interrupted her: "But you ... where did you get this knife? Did you take it from him? He didn't stab you, did he?"

Silence fell again until Diana called out indignantly, "Let me go!" Presumably her husband was checking her for injuries. I had the impression that he'd found none, at least he mentioned nothing that would have indicated that.

"That doesn't make any sense," Pearl said. "Some man is supposed to have attacked Diana? And she stabbed him? Who the hell are they talking about?"

"The knife," Diana repeated like a sleepwalker. "The knife, oh God, I have no idea where it came from. I can't remember. I ... was asleep. Then something woke me up. I don't know what it was. A noise, maybe? It was pitch black, but I felt someone leaning over me. I could feel his breath. Then there was a blow to my head. And after that ... I don't remember anything."

"The knife," Sendrik insisted, "how did it get into your room? The blade is bloody, don't you see? And he has the matching stab wound in his stomach; it killed him, as far as I can see."

Presumably he was pointing to the corpse with these words, but he still did not mention the man's name. It made you want to jump out of your fur!

"Diana," Sendrik said then, in what seemed to me an anxiously calm tone. "Have you been drinking again?"

"No!" she cried.

To which he simply replied: "Don't lie to me, I can smell it on your breath!"

"I ... it was really just one glass," she protested. "Before bed. A nightcap!"

I could hear her bursting into tears again at these words.

She gave an agonized sob and shrieked, "Oh God, I killed him! Did I really kill him?"

Her voice shifted, became hysterical. "I will go to prison. To the madhouse!"

"Diana, please calm down!" cried Sendrik.

"But it was self-defense, wasn't it?" she continued to howl. "It must have been self-defense. Why would I ... I would never ... I'm not violent, am I, darling?"

"No..." he said, albeit rather hesitantly, "you're not."

Again there was a short silence, then Sendrik continued in a more controlled manner: "He attacked you and knocked you down, you say. With what? I don't see a weapon anywhere here. Apart from the knife you..."

"I really don't know!" Diana exclaimed. "I don't know anything anymore. Please help me ... what is happening to me? Am I completely losing my mind?"

"No, honey ... take it easy. Breathe, you have to

breathe, dear. In and out ... just calm down. Yes, that's it, you're doing great. Don't stop."

A minute or two passed, then Diana said—now in a more composed fashion: "It felt like a blow, not a stab. And I don't have a cut, do I?"

Her composure was already gone again. "Oh God, Sendrik!" she sobbed out anew. "They're going to lock me up. I can't take that, I won't survive! Will I go to an asylum, a closed institution?"

"Diana, please, you need to calm down. We can do this, okay? No one is going to lock you up. You have to be strong. Think about Juno. She needs you."

"But how ... what are we going to do?"

"Let me think!"

There was an even longer pause than before, then Sendrik said, "Come into the bathroom first so we can clean you up. The blood has to go. And after that I have an idea already, I think ..."

We learned no more, because now the two of them had run into the bathroom and we could not hear anything further.

"So what now?" said Pearl. "Should we make a noise? Get the humans out of bed so they can find the body before these two make it disappear?"

"Let's go get Victoria," I suggested. "But we have to take good care of her so she doesn't get attacked."

"We'll do that," Pearl said in a grandiose tone of voice, as if *she* were the one who would be doing the protecting.

We ran back to our room, and before I could wake

125

our human with a gentle lick, Pearl had already jumped onto the bed and slapped one of her paws right into Victoria's face. Fortunately her paws were small, but even a tiny cat like Pearl already possessed fairly sharp claws—which, when she was very excited, she often extended without thinking of the consequences.

Victoria woke from her sleep with a startled cry.

"Do you always have to be so brutal?" I accused Pearl.

"No time for tenderness," she answered. "Go ahead and do your barking-and-running-to-the-door thingy so she knows to come along."

I put the insult away without comment and did as I was told. The way Pearl made it sound, my tried-and-true method of communication—one of the very few we had at our disposal to relate anything to Victoria—sounded downright banal.

Well, anyway, I managed to direct Victoria to Diana's room, where she knocked on the door, first cautiously, then a little more insistently.

Finally Diana opened the door to her. She was wearing a pristine, white, spotless nightgown that gave off the smell of fresh laundry, while the room was clearly reeking of blood.

However, there was nothing to be seen that would have been conspicuous in any way; no traces of blood, no knife and certainly no corpse.

Sendrik had also disappeared. We were too late. Had he simply dumped the dead body conveniently over the terrace? With some strength—which I believed

Sendrik had—and a lot of momentum, he might have been able to hurl the corpse into the depths in such a way that it would not have come to rest on the narrow ridge under Diana's terrace, but dropped into the abyss right away.

I was not so sure about that, because the ridge was a few meters wide. I did not have the opportunity to run out onto the balcony and check whether perhaps another dead body was lying down below on the gravel—which could then be disposed of later in the ravine—because the terrace door was locked.

Had Dr. Bachmann died and been disposed of in a similar way to the newly dead man, still unknown to us? And were there now—or at any rate soon to be—already two corpses lying in the gorge or on the steep slopes of its flanks?

Victoria stood there embarrassed, not really knowing what to do. She didn't understand why I had led her here to Diana in the middle of the night.

"Are you all right?" she asked her friend.

Diana still smelled scared and her eyes looked red, but she put on a surprisingly good act. "Yes ... why?" she asked in the tone of an innocent angel. "What's wrong?"

"I don't know," Victoria said. She gave me a stern look. "Athos raised the alarm and directed me here..."

"Strange," Diana commented.

Oh, what a hypocrite!

That was the end of the matter for Victoria. She apologized to her client for the night's disturbance, I earned another stern look from her, and then we returned to our suite with Pearl.

19

The next morning, the kitten and I set out to find all the occupants of the house. We were desperate to know who was missing—who that body that had been dumped by Diana and Sendrik the previous night could be. There had been talk of a 'he,' so we looked around for the men first.

We roamed around the castle, peering into the rooms whose doors I could open or which were ajar, tracking down more and more of the two-leggeds.

However, three people remained hidden from us: among the men that included Bastian Leonhardt and Chris Wieland. We could not find them in the park, either, but from this we could not immediately draw the worst conclusion.

Both men's rooms had doorknobs fitted, which I could not open even after several attempts. There were so many different styles and building eras represented in the castle that almost every door looked different, and there were also many different types of handles. In both cases Pearl scratched at the door while I barked loudly to attract the attention of Bastian and Chris respectively, but we were not admitted.

"Let's try again later," I said to Pearl. "Maybe they are late risers."

The tiny one made a frowning face. "Bastian…. It would fit if he had been killed, don't you think? He was after Diana—even Sendrik knew that. Maybe Bastian crept into her room last night to seduce her ... but she had no desire for him?"

"Possibly," I said. "But he was—he is—Sendrik's brother, after all. So would Sendrik have made him disappear so easily, without shedding a tear for him, if Diana had killed him?"

"Brothers or not, those two can't stand each other," Pearl pointed out. She was right, of course.

The third person we couldn't track down was Juno. She was not a man, but we were still worried about her. She was very rich, as we had since found out, and her boyfriend was in desperate need of money. Barbara was currently managing her assets, but only as long as Juno did not marry.

Juno's constitution was so weak that it certainly wouldn't have taken much to send her to the afterlife.

None of the humans we met said a word about what was going on with Juno, and of course we couldn't ask them about her. Was she suffering the effects of her illness again and therefore still lying in bed?

The door to her suite of rooms had a handle that could be pushed down, but it was locked. That could mean that Juno wasn't there—but where was she, then? She could hardly have gone for a long walk through the park, or have left the castle to indulge in some typically teenage activity.

The other possibility was that she had locked her door from the inside and was simply fast asleep. Or that she didn't want to receive any visitors—not even

Pearl and me. We made our presence felt outside her door, as we had tried to do with Bastian and Chris, but our efforts were not to be crowned with success here either.

Finally Pearl made a completely crazy suggestion: "Let's go to the library and question the ghost girl. She might just be the perfect witness—after all, she can roam anywhere in the house unseen, can't she? Ghosts can walk through walls; you see that a lot in scary movies."

"And you think that's true?"

"Why not?" said Pearl. "It would be logical, wouldn't it? After all, ghosts don't have bodies anymore, and I don't think they need sleep either, because they often haunt houses at night. That girl might have seen something. Maybe she knows who was murdered last night ... and by whom."

Apparently the pipsqueak had now become an expert on the supernatural. That was all I needed.

"We know by *whom* he was murdered," I objected. "By Diana."

"All right," Pearl agreed. "But did she bump him off in cold blood, or was she just defending herself? Then she would be the victim, and he the perpetrator."

"True, that," I grumbled.

I felt little desire for another encounter with the belligerent girl in the library, whatever it might actually be. Ghost, hallucination...

Somebody who threw books at my head, and hated dogs, was in any case not my friend!

"A ghost as a witness?" I said to Pearl. "I really don't know if that's a wise idea."

"Why not? A good detective uses every available resource. Even if it may be a little ... well, unusual."

"Unusual?" I growled. But my protest was ignored, as so often happened.

Pearl prevailed by simply stomping off in the direction of the library, and I had no choice but to follow her. I had to keep an eye on her, my little super detective and, lately, ghost whisperer. If the girl in the library got the idea of throwing books at the midget too, it could end badly. Pearl didn't have my robust build, which would only suffer a few—albeit painful—bumps from such an attack.

When we reached the library and I opened the door for us, Pearl held me back.

"I'd better go in alone," she suggested. "I don't think our spirit is too fond of dogs. Will you wait out here and keep an eye on me?"

I agreed—and lay in wait on the doorstep.

Pearl trudged bravely into the room. She looked around, sniffed, probably let her sixth cat sense pick up the scent or whatever, and after a long time of running around and calling in a friendly fashion, finally came to stand in front of one of the floor-to-ceiling bookshelves. Or rather, she sat down on her hindquarters and stared up at the shelves.

What was she seeing there? The ghost?

I myself again perceived only a shadow, and even that might just have been only a figment of my imagination. I barely trusted my own senses any more, on which I had always relied so completely. Perhaps dogs—and cats—fell victim to delusions to the same extent as our two-legged friends. A sobering thought, but I could not shake it off.

Carefully, I crawled a little closer to Pearl. She didn't seem to notice. I concentrated on what she was saying to the ghost she seemed to be communicating with.

"Wait," she was just meowing, "so you're saying you loved spooky stories—when you were alive—but don't feel like doing any haunting yourself now that you've become a ghost?"

The shadow appeared to agree with her; at least that's how it seemed to me.

"But that's ... well, it's pretty unusual," Pearl said. "Kind of crazy. What? No, no, I'm sorry, I didn't mean to imply that I thought you were insane."

The conversation continued to develop, and I had the impression that Pearl and the ghost girl—whom I could only distinguish as a dark shadow today—were increasingly trusting each other.

But as for myself, I had the feeling that the phantom was sending me a very clear message: "Don't come any closer, dog."

So I stayed where I was, determined not to take the vituperation personally.

The longer Pearl and the ghost spoke with each other, the more I had the impression that I could not only understand Pearl's questions, but increasingly also the answers she was receiving.

Advancing delusions? That could not be ruled out. Nevertheless, I pricked up my ears and listened.

"I love the Wednesday Evening Club," the ghost now seemed to say. "Always have, even when I was still able to attend in the flesh. I always looked forward to it all week, and I spent every spare moment here in the library between meetings, too. I just couldn't get enough of the exciting ghost stories. That's why I stayed in the castle, even after I died. But doing any haunting by yourself is just boring; reading is much better."

Then, a little later, I had the feeling that the conversation had finally turned to Juno.

"Maybe she will soon be my friend," said the ghost, "as sick as she is. I'm sure she'll die soon, and then I won't be alone any longer. She loves books in general and the Wednesday Evening Club in particular as much as I do, it seems to me. Oh, we'll have lots of fun together! Do you think I'll have to wait much longer for her to die?" she asked Pearl.

The midget was overwhelmed by this outrageous question. She let out an indignant meow, then tried to explain to the ghost that one should not simply wish for the death of a human being.

The girl, however, was intransigent. She seemed to be interested only in her own dreams and wishes. Finally she said to Pearl, "Are you going to stay here in the castle, too? I've never had a pet, you know..."

"I'm sorry," Pearl said firmly, "but my human and my dog need me."

Then the shadow disappeared, and I heard nothing more. The library looked like an ordinary, albeit gloomy place again, and not as if it had sprung straight out of a horror story. It became brighter in the room—yes, really!—and warmer, it seemed to me.

Pearl called after the ghost, "Wait! You have to help us! Can you tell me if Juno is in danger? And did you perhaps see or hear anything last night..."

But her words seemed to crash against an invisible wall of silence. The ghost was gone; mission failed.

Pearl dropped to the floor in frustration and began an all-out fur cleaning spree. I rushed to her side.

"Such a rude brat," she scolded, "to disappear without a word! And she'd really be quite happy to see Juno murdered—just so she can have some company. A ghost who won't haunt, but loves hauntings. She's nuts!"

So I had not imagined the girl's words, or at least Pearl and I had suffered the same delusion. What a consolation...

Only a short while later, a horrible thought came to me—which I immediately shared with Pearl.

"Do you think the ghost girl could hurt Juno?" I asked. "Just so she can finally have a friend?"

Pearl's eyes widened. "What, but ... a ghost can't commit murder. Or can they?"

"I don't know. She can throw books, that much we know. Maybe she could use a knife, too? Or some other weapon."

I didn't hear what Pearl said, because at that moment

a strange feeling came over me. I suddenly had the image of the ghost girl in front of me again, but now only in my mind's eye. At the same time, however, I was seized by the firm conviction that I had seen this castle ghost, this selfish little girl somewhere before.

But *where*? I just couldn't figure it out, no matter how hard I tried.

20

In the afternoon, Pearl and I decided to roam the castle again to look for Bastian, Chris and Juno, but we didn't get far with our search.

On the ground floor—where we'd just begun our tour—we met Victoria, who was entering one of the smaller salons. Loud voices could be heard from there, and our human was probably curious about what kind of argument was going on in that room.

"Pronounced snooping instincts," Pearl once again commented with satisfaction on the behavior of our two-legged.

The small salon that Victoria had entered—and we with her, of course—was decorated entirely in black and white. At first glance one had a strong impression of having strayed onto a chessboard.

Sendrik was sitting on a snow-white sofa, with a newspaper beside him and a whiskey glass in his right hand. Barbara was standing in front of him, and seemed very determined to prevent him from drinking.

"Really, Sendrik, I have to wonder!" she exclaimed in a querulous voice. "You're already getting drunk at this hour? Isn't it enough for you that your wife is addicted to alcohol?"

"W-what?" stammered Sendrik. He was probably too stunned to come up with an appropriate retort to put

Barbara in her place.

"You two are miserable role models for Juno!" she continued, with equal zeal. "What do you want her to become one day? A chronic drunkard?"

"Barbara, you're really going too far—"

She didn't seem to be hearing his objections at all.

"I would strongly suggest that from now on all alcohol be banned from this house," she hurled at him. "And that's not a request!"

With these words she whirled around, ran without a greeting past Victoria, who had stopped near the door, and rushed out of the room.

Sendrik sat transfixed for a moment, then slowly raised his whiskey glass to his lips and emptied it with an emphatically gleeful expression. The anger that was boiling inside him wafted to my nose as an acrid smell.

"That old hag," he hissed, then put on an apologetic smile. "Victoria ... what must you think of us? Would you like a drink, perhaps? Ha! While I can still offer you one," he added with a bitter smile.

Victoria declined with thanks. "Barbara may be concerned about Juno," she said, "but a blanket ban on alcohol throughout the house? For everyone? That does seem a little radical to me."

"You can say that again!" Sendrik exclaimed. "She's not right in the head, that old woman. Maybe you can give *her* some therapy!"

He laughed throatily. "No, she would never let that happen. She thinks she's perfect, that old house dragon!"

Victoria sat down on the black armchair that stood to the left of Sendrik's snow-white sofa.

"It's none of my business," she began hesitantly, "but why do you put up with such treatment? Wouldn't it be better for you not to live under the same roof as Barbara?"

"Ha!" replied Sendrik, "it's her house we're staying in, just in case you don't know. And Diana won't leave it at any price. Neither will Juno."

"*Her* house?" Victoria repeated incredulously.

"Well, it's actually Juno's house. She inherited it from her late father, along with the rest of his estate. He owned everything you see here. His family has lived in this castle for generations ... and has amassed considerable assets. Well, anyway, Barbara manages everything for now, until Juno's eighteenth birthday. Or until her wedding, should she get married before then."

"Good heavens," Victoria snapped. "Now that's a ... well, a very unusual will."

"Indeed. And it probably won't surprise you that it was Barbara who talked her brother—Juno's father—into this arrangement. She insisted that Juno must be provided for, and that Diana would only squander his millions away. She never liked my wife. And Alexander listened to her—I don't know why."

"Unbelievable," Victoria muttered.

"Excellent, now she finally knows," Pearl commented. But then she gave me a questioning look. "Does it even matter for our case anymore?"

"Which case do you mean, now?" I returned, frustrated. "The dead doctor that no one is even talking about anymore? The dead guy from last night, whom we still haven't identified? Diana might have imagined him, but surely Sendrik didn't. He's still in his right mind—at least I hope so. Or do you mean Juno, who is perhaps being taken advantage of by her boyfriend—or even worse—maybe he wants to marry her to inherit her fortune? Or perhaps her aunt is out to get her because she's embezzled some of Juno's money. And then we have the dog-hating ghost girl who would love to have a playmate ... so, which case are we talking about exactly?"

"I don't know," Pearl grumbled.

"And you can't do anything about this arrangement?" Victoria enquired of Sendrik. "It seems to me that Barbara is abusing her power, and that can't really be in Juno's best interest."

"What should we do, in your opinion?" Sendrik replied. "Challenge Alexander's will? Should Diana perhaps sue her daughter, who is the heiress after all? And what can we bring against Barbara as the executor of the estate? That she's a toxic old woman who bullies all of us—while she's absolutely obsessed with Juno?"

He shook his head. "No, we can live with it; we have to. I make enough money myself, so that's not the point. My clinic in Bolzano is still smallish, but I can't complain ... and this madness has an expiration date. Maybe we'll be able to get rid of Barbara very soon, if Juno really wants to marry Daniel. And otherwise we'll get through the two years as best we can. Juno won't kick her out of the house in any case, once she gets full control of her assets; she has too good a heart to do that. But at least Barbara won't be allowed to act like the castle's mistress anymore, who could put us all out to pasture if we don't live up to her antiquated moral standards." He pressed his lips together resolutely.

Victoria returned a silent nod.

"Actually, one might even feel sorry for her," Sendrik continued. "Barbara, I mean. She seriously thinks she's doing all of this for the good of the child. She really is morbidly infatuated with Juno, if you ask me."

He shrugged. "She could definitely use a therapist—although I'd fully understand it if you wouldn't want to take on such a patient."

"Is it possible that Barbara is opposing Juno's marriage to Daniel because of this?" our blossoming assistant detective asked. "Because she would then lose control of the fortune?"

"You bet," Sendrik said. "Aside from the fact that Daniel isn't good enough as a husband for her beloved Juno. She hates him—as she hates virtually everyone except Juno."

Victoria folded her hands in her lap. She looked reluctant, and started talking about how she would like to ask a somewhat delicate question.

"Go ahead," Sendrik said. "As you can see, I'm used to a harsh tone ... and to sharp criticism."

"Oh, it's nothing like that," Victoria said quickly. "I don't mean to criticize you, far be it from me. I was just wondering who would actually inherit if Juno—well, if she succumbed to her illness. That's not out of the question, is it? It seems to me she's in a very bad way."

Sendrik's features darkened, but not because the question angered him. He seemed to be blaming himself for Juno's suffering.

"I just can't stand being so helpless and having to watch her experience such agony every day," he said. "I always thought of myself as a dedicated and very passable doctor, but with her..."

He shook his head. "That's where I've failed across the board."

"I'm sorry," Victoria said. "I didn't mean to..."

"That's all right. You really don't have to apologize. To return to your question: should Juno actually pass away, the remaining fortune would go to Diana. That's what Alexander stipulated in his will. It seems to me that he was also a very stubborn man, and that at least on that point he defied his crazy sister."

"So Diana would inherit everything," Victoria muttered to herself. Her brow furrowed; she seemed to be thinking hard about the matter. "And Barbara would no longer have any rights as trustee in that case, either."

"That's right," Sendrik confirmed.

"Is it a large sum, then? Apart from this castle, which alone must be worth a fortune—forgive me for asking so indiscreetly."

Sendrik nodded. "No problem. And yes, we're talking hundreds of millions in securities and savings deposits alone. But what are you getting at?"

His expression suddenly darkened further. "That Juno could be in danger because of this money? Threatened by my wife, because she wants to get hold of the fortune? You can't be serious!"

He did not give Victoria a chance to answer him.

"You're barking up the wrong tree on this one," he exclaimed. "Diana may have her problems, I won't deny that, but she loves her daughter! Not as foppishly as Barbara does, but no less so because of it. She would never harm a hair on Juno's head!"

"Of course not," Victoria said quickly. "I certainly didn't mean to imply that. It's just..."

"Yes? Speak to me plainly," Sendrik said, but not as kindly as before.

"The disappearance of Dr. Bachmann ... it just won't stop bothering me. I wonder if he might not have found something out."

"Found out what?"

"About Juno, I mean. About her health," Victoria said cautiously.

"Hmm. Well, I really can't imagine—I may not be an eminent expert like him, seeing as I'm just a cosmetic doctor, but I assure you that since I married Diana I've studied Juno's ailments, her symptoms, her episodes of illness very closely. I may not be able to cure her, but I am sure that no one is doing her any harm. I would never overlook that! Never!"

Victoria nodded slowly, but she didn't really look convinced.

"As for Dr. Bachmann," Sendrik continued, "I would

imagine that Barbara got on his nerves very quickly. As I told you, she hired him explicitly to drive Daniel away with a particularly grim health prognosis for Juno—and knowing Barbara, she had no patience with him whatsoever. She certainly demanded concrete results from Dr. Bachmann after only a few days, nagging him all the while ... and he, unlike us, didn't have to put up with it. He's a capable doctor who can easily find patients, who will treat him with respect, without any trouble."

"Yes, that would be quite a plausible explanation," Victoria said. She shrugged apologetically. "I guess I worry too much."

"Not at all," Sendrik replied. "You're a smart woman and very concerned about Diana. I appreciate that. Please continue to keep your eyes open, okay? It may sound paranoid, but it's always better to be safe than sorry."

21

At dinner we finally learned who the dead man in Diana's room had been.

Bastian Leonhardt, whom we had not been able to find all day, was one of the first to appear at the table. Juno entered the room shortly behind him, leaning on Barbara's arm.

"Oh, how nice, are you feeling better?" Victoria said by way of comment on her appearance, and Juno nodded with a cautious smile on her lips.

But the one who didn't show up for dinner was Chris Wieland, Juno's teacher. It was she who pointed out his absence.

"Where is Mr. Wieland tonight?" she asked. "It must be the first time he's ever been late for dinner."

"This would be the first time he's ever been late for anything," Barbara corrected her. Apparently, the household tyrant seemed to hold the teacher in high regard—a distinction he certainly hadn't earned lightly.

"It's the weekend," Daniel, who was once again a guest at the castle, interposed. "That's when Mr. Wieland has his days off. So maybe he's gone into town, or even treated himself to a little weekend trip?"

Barbara screwed up her face. "Without signing off? I really couldn't imagine that."

"So is this a military base now?" Daniel whispered in

his sweetheart's ear. *"Report for duty to Sergeant Barbara!"* He spoke softly enough so that the old woman could not hear him, but his words did not escape me.

Juno had to grin, and gave him a quick kiss. But then her mood turned serious again. "Could someone check on Mr. Wieland, please? His car is outside in the parking lot, so I can't imagine he's gone to town."

Pearl and I had already suspected it, and shortly thereafter it was proved horribly true for the two-leggeds as well: Chris Wieland was dead. Barbara went to check on him at Juno's request and found his body on the bed in his room.

It appeared he had stabbed himself, but Pearl and I knew better, of course. He had to be the man who'd met his death in Diana's room the previous night, because none of the castle's inhabitants were now missing except for him.

Sendrik had apparently transported his body back to his room last night, and then tried to feign suicide— for the knife with which Wieland had been killed was now stuck in the stomach wound, and the tutor's right hand was lying limp around the handle of the weapon.

What surprised Pearl and me, however, was that a sheet of paper with extremely strange notes had been found on Wieland's desk. They were written in spidery handwriting, as if they had been jotted down by a madman.

Victoria, who had come into the room with us and the other two-leggeds after Barbara had discovered the body, read the lines:

There is no cure for lycanthropy.
I must not endanger my beloved.

"Lycanthro.... What is that?" sniffled Juno, leaning heavily on Daniel's arm and crying big tears.

"The transformation of a human into a werewolf," Daniel explained to her.

"Our current topic at the Wednesday Evening Club," Barbara murmured. She was chalk white and for once didn't seem eager to take the helm. Faced with the dead man, she was just as perplexed as everyone else.

"He killed himself because he was afraid he would turn into a werewolf?" Bastian asked incredulously. "That can't be true! Was he insane?"

He looked at Victoria as if, in her role as a psychotherapist, she must have an answer to his question.

"Chris wasn't my client," she said, "and I barely knew him. But for what it's worth, he seemed very quiet and introverted. Of course, that could have just been his nature—but maybe we should have interpreted it as a sign of depressive illness."

She looked first at Barbara, then at Juno. "Had he been acting strangely in the last few weeks, or months? Did he seem changed?"

Both Barbara and Juno assured her that Mr. Wieland had been 'just as usual'.

"The note must be fake!" Pearl murmured to me. "We know he didn't kill himself."

"But he could very well have gone mad," I posited. "Everything points to that, doesn't it? I mean, if he crept into Diana's room in the middle of the night and attacked her.... Who knows, maybe he really believed himself to be dangerous, and was thinking of the werewolf character that was the subject of the last Wednesday Evening Club session. Or rather, from the looks of it, Chris was *indeed* dangerous."

Even as I was giving Pearl this attempt at an explanation, something occurred to me: "That wolf howl we heard," I cried, "the other night when Dr. Bachmann was murdered—do you remember that it made no sense at all?"

"Sure," Pearl agreed, "that was really creepy ... but what about it? What does that have to do with the death of the two-legged teacher?"

"Well, nothing maybe. Possibly everything, though. What if they were not ordinary wolves? Surely there aren't packs that big around here."

"What are you getting at, Athos?" Pearl looked at me as if I were also on the verge of losing my mind.

I didn't beat around the bush any longer: "Werewolves!" I exclaimed. "What if it was werewolves that we heard? Humans who had turned into wolves and were talking crazy because of it—in the language of wolves, but with no real sense or reason!"

A cold lump formed in my throat as I was explaining this crazy theory to Pearl; I did not recognize myself anymore. I have always been a sensible dog, just as my first human, Professor Adler, raised me to be. To him science had been everything. *He* would certainly not have believed in werewolves.

And in truth, I didn't either! I was just ... well, I was

pretty rattled. And could I be blamed for it, after all that had already happened in this haunted castle? Would I also end up going mad and throwing myself into the abyss—as Dr. Bachmann may well have done? Had both Chris and the doctor been out of their minds? Had the doctor committed suicide, just like the poor guy in Wednesday night's story, who had also ended his life by jumping off a cliff? The similarity had just struck me now.

22

I shook myself to clear my head.

"Pearl, do you think I've been acting a bit strangely the past few days?" I addressed the midget with concern.

She looked at me uncomprehendingly. "No stranger than usual. Just like a dog," she said in her inimitably charming way. "Why do you ask?"

She examined me with her baby-blue eyes, from which shone an oh-so-innocent look.

"I ... don't know," I said, "the thought of those werewolves ... I think I'm going to lose it."

"Well, I'm not a wolf expert," Pearl said, "but that howling the other day, those weren't people turning into wolves. Those were real wolves ... even if they were spouting complete nonsense."

She sat up straight and wrapped her tail around her hind paws—one of her thinking poses.

While the humans in the room were engaging in a heated debate about Chris Wieland's state of mind and deliberating what to do next, Pearl seemed to sink into a state of deep musing.

Finally she raised her head, giving me another piercing baby-blue look, and then she said: "Well, in TV crime shows it's always the case that behind every seemingly supernatural event there's a human agent in the end—usually the murderer."

"There are no real ghosts in those shows either," I objected. "But there is one here in the castle: that girl in the library. We've both seen and heard her. She's real—you don't doubt that, do you?"

"No," Pearl had to admit. "But that doesn't make the werewolves real, does it? What if a human was behind the wolf howls? Someone could have just played the sounds, couldn't they? Over a loudspeaker?"

"Pearl, you're a genius!" escaped my lips—although I had already sworn several times not to praise the tiny one anymore. She was already sufficiently full of herself, I thought.

Even now she didn't react in surprise, but merely looked pleased. "Yeah? You think so?" Actually, it sounded less like a question and more like benevolent praise that I had recognized her superior intelligence.

But I was much too excited to resent her.

"Think about it!" I exclaimed. "Humans don't understand the language of wolves. If some two-legged uses a recording of wolves howling, it may have been made anywhere in the world. At a time for example, when it was bitterly cold, in winter, and in a region where wolves still hunt reindeer or are threatened by mountain lions. Do you understand? No human would have noticed that the howling that night was completely inappropriate. Only us! But nobody cares about that."

The howling of the wolves had apparently come from one of the terraces, or even the roof—which should have put me on the right track right away. After all, wolves do not climb buildings.

Sometimes I really am slow on the uptake.

Someone had probably placed a loudspeaker or cell phone on one of the terraces above us, and it had played the wolf howl at a predetermined time. Bastian, for example—he lived on the second floor. Had he tried to drive someone crazy with the howling?

"So I was right," Pearl commented on my explanation. "It was an audio recording and not a real pack meeting!"

"Apparently, several recordings of different wolf packs were randomly pieced together," I said. "One was from a group that went reindeer hunting, and a second was from the wolves that had a mountain lion problem. We really should have figured that one out ... instead of being intimidated by some werewolf legends!"

"*You* believed in the werewolves," Pearl said. "I didn't. And I certainly wasn't intimidated!"

I let my tail hang. I had been blind, stupid and naive. But Pearl did not go any further into my self-criticism, but rather picked up on our new realization.

"All right," she said in a professional investigator's tone, "then someone here in the house wants to drive the other two-leggeds crazy. But why? Is he himself completely out of his mind? And who is his victim? Diana? Remember when we arrived here at the castle— she heard a werewolf, too. One that was supposedly in its death throes, and the sound was coming from under her bed. That could have been a recording as well. Someone's trying to drive the poor woman mad,

Athos!"

"Looks like it."

"And on the night when Dr. Bachmann died, this same someone played the wolf's howl on the terrace above Diana's room in order to lure her out onto the balcony. And there, down on the narrow ridge, she was to discover the doctor's body—which disappeared immediately afterwards. And that made Diana doubt her sanity all the more."

"Bastian is in love with Diana," I said. "And—wait a minute. Remember he was suddenly in the stairwell, running to Diana, when she heard the wolf howl, saw the body, and cried out?"

"Well sure, he almost stamped me flat! Why?"

"What if he didn't come down from above, but merely pretended to, making a quick about-face when he saw us so that Victoria would think he was coming from upstairs? In truth, he might have just run up the stairs from below, having pushed the doctor's body into the ravine under Diana's balcony. He could have programmed the wolf howl upstairs to go off at a specific time. He didn't have to be on the second floor to do that. Something like that is not a problem for modern cell phones."

"Wow, yeah, that sounds crazy. But it is plausible," Pearl agreed.

"What if Bastian only wants Diana to *believe* she's crazy ... and then plays her comforter, confidant or savior so she finally falls in love with him? And leaves the castle with him?"

"Hmm," Pearl murmured. "But was Wieland in love with Diana, too—just like Bastian? Or who might be the sweetheart referred to in that scrawled message on his table?"

"If he even wrote that himself," I mused. "Maybe Sendrik forged that note afterwards to make the suicide look believable."

Pearl groaned. "Soon I'll be losing my mind with all the machinations of these crazy two-leggeds," she complained.

"And that's not all," I said. "Who killed Dr. Bachmann? Or was he also driven mad and thus plunged into the abyss of his own accord?"

"Hmm," Pearl said, "you found that button from his jacket in Diana's bedroom. And Chris died in the same place, also there by Diana. Somehow she seems to have been involved in both deaths. What if we're meowing up the wrong tree with Bastian as a suspect, and Diana is actually the crazy one and murdered both men?"

"And her motive?" I asked.

"Insane serial killers don't need a motive," Pearl said. "You should know that, my dear colleague."

23

This time, the two-leggeds had no choice but to call the police. Even Barbara—always concerned about the family's reputation—realized that Chris Wieland's death could not simply be swept under the rug.

Two police officers arrived; one of them seemed to be clearly above the other in rank, and he was apparently well acquainted with the family. The man's name was known in the castle, or at least he did not introduce himself when he appeared. Sendrik addressed him as "Esposito," and I assumed that was his last name.

He looked as if he was already approaching retirement, and had hardly any hair left on his head, but he had a wise pair of eyes and a few kind words for Pearl and me when he came into the castle—which gave him a good start in gaining our sympathy right away.

Esposito treated Sendrik, who had taken over contact with the police, in a decidedly polite manner, dropping a remark about how his wife, Gerda, was really pleased with her new nose. "She's already saving up for a—what's the word?—a complete makeover at your clinic, you know," Esposito said.

Sendrik nodded, but really didn't seem to be in the mood to talk about his services as a plastic surgeon at the moment. He led the two policemen to Chris Wieland's room, while Pearl and I followed the men unobtrusively.

Fortunately, as pets we were once again unchallenged, whereas a two-legged would have caused a stir and been chased away as an overly curious snoop. So we could follow the police investigation—albeit from a distance.

We weren't allowed into the dead man's room of course, but the door remained open behind Sendrik and the two policemen, and we could listen and peer in from the corridor.

Esposito first thoroughly inspected the corpse, then looked at the scrawled message about turning into a werewolf.

"Poor guy," he said to Sendrik, "he seems to have completely lost it." He tapped his index finger against his temple. "I guess the atmosphere in your old haunted castle did him no good in the long run. No offense, Dr. Leonhardt," he added quickly.

He then took out his cell phone, had a conversation in Italian that I couldn't understand, and finally asked Sendrik to take a seat downstairs in the salon, where the other residents had gathered. The investigation would take some time, and civilians were not allowed to be present, he explained in an almost obsequious tone.

Sendrik had no problem with that. He seemed to me rather happy to be allowed to leave the dead man's room.

A good hour passed before two more plainclothes police officers arrived and went upstairs.

The castle residents and the guests, including Victoria, spent the time almost wordlessly in the ground floor salon.

Pearl and I, who had kept roaming around the house so as not to miss any of the police investigation, stopped by the salon twice, and each time we were met with a grave silence.

Some of the two-leggeds were drinking coffee, Diana and Sendrik were indulging in whiskey, and not even Barbara had objected to this alcohol consumption tonight—even if she herself was sitting stiff as a wooden doll and nursing a glass of warm milk.

Finally, the inspector or commissioner—or whatever his title might have been—came into the salon and indicated to Sendrik with a nod of his head that he would like to speak to him outside the door. Apparently what he had to say was not meant for the ears of just anyone.

Sendrik jumped to his feet. Pearl and I rose as well—as inconspicuously as possible. I stretched extensively and then strolled out into the hallway close behind Sendrik, as if I had just awakened from a deep sleep and was now longing to move my paws a bit.

Pearl yawned so demonstratively that she received an "Oh, how cute!" from Esposito, which she registered with some satisfaction. It was clearly unacceptable that someone should not comment on what a delightful creature she was.

Cats....

But back to the topic: we both followed Sendrik and Esposito out into the hallway. The two of them moved a little distance away from the door of the salon; apparently the inspector really wanted to make sure that no one in the room could follow their conversation.

Finally he stopped and shuffled nervously from one leg to the other.

"We found something, Dr. Leonhardt," he began hesitantly. "Something you should know about."

Sendrik looked surprised. "Yes? What?"

"We checked the dead man's cell phone; purely routine in a suspicious death, you understand. Fortunately he had facial recognition activated, which made our job a lot easier—compared to ordinary password protection, I mean. Even a dead person can still give us access to his data this way. But that's not the point. My colleague went through the phone, looking at the emails, chat messages, photo albums and social media apps that were available. Suicides sometimes announce their intent, you know—with a message to their friends, or even publicly on one of their social media profiles."

"And did Mr. Wieland do that?" asked Sendrik. "Did he post anywhere that he was going to harm himself?"

He really was a good actor. His words came across as sincerely concerned, although he knew full well that the tutor had not killed himself.

"He didn't," Esposito said, "but we found something else on his cell phone, something that could match his cryptic goodbye message to the loved one he didn't want to endanger."

"Oh?" Sendrik said, astonished. Maybe he wasn't such an outstanding actor as I had assumed.

Again Esposito shifted from one leg to the other. I could smell how uncomfortable he was. Whatever he had to tell Sendrik seemed to be making him very anxious indeed.

"We found photos of your stepdaughter on Chris Wieland's cell phone," Esposito finally said, avoiding Sendrik's gaze. "They were taken last night in Juno's bedroom, I think—probably just before Mr. Wieland took his own life. We have yet to determine his exact time of death, but I'm guessing it was around midnight, give or take an hour or two. If it's all right with you, we'd like to look at Juno's bedroom to confirm that the pictures were taken there. Anyway, she's in bed in the photos and—"

"Good God!" Sendrik interrupted him. "You mean ... please tell me he didn't..."

"No," Esposito said quickly. "I don't think he sexually assaulted her. It looks more like he was just watching over her and snapping these photos. While she was sleeping, you know?"

Sendrik gasped. "Then he was ... then our Juno is the sweetheart he alluded to in his scribblings? He was in love with my stepdaughter?"

He wiped his forehead with his shirt sleeve, then continued haltingly, "Wieland ... has been in this house for years, teaching Juno since she was ten or eleven. Diana's late husband hired him, you know. After all, I've only been married to her for less than a year."

"I knew Mr. Messner well," Esposito said.

Then he sought Sendrik's gaze. "Would you mind if we asked Juno a few questions? Whether she noticed any of these ... feelings that her tutor seemed to have for her—whether he ever approached her? Of course, you could be there for the interview," he added quickly. "Or your wife; whatever you think is better."

"I'll take care of this," Sendrik said. "My wife is ... a little mentally unstable at the moment, I'm afraid. And I can count on you not to upset Juno with your questions? You'll have to be extremely gentle."

"Of course," Esposito promised him.

Sendrik fetched his stepdaughter from the salon. Daniel wanted to accompany her, but Sendrik turned him away. "This is a private family matter," he explained to him.

Pearl had no trouble getting Juno's attention when she entered the hallway, leaning on her stepfather's arm. The kitten sank her miniature teeth into one of Juno's trouser legs, playfully pulling on it and meowing sweetly.

Juno smiled and promptly asked her stepfather to pick up the midget for her. He did, and she took Pearl in her free arm.

Together with Esposito, the father, stepdaughter and cat went into a smaller reading room. I tried to follow them unobtrusively, but the door was shut in my face as they entered the room.

Annoying, but at least Pearl was in the room and could follow the conversation.

Afterwards, she told me everything she had picked up, so that I can report on it here:

Esposito proceeded very cautiously, as promised. He first asked Juno whether or not *someone* might have entered her room last night when she was already in bed. He did not give a name.

Juno replied in the affirmative. "I wasn't feeling so great yesterday," she explained to him, "so I wasn't at dinner, and on such occasions the others usually check on me before bed."

"'The others'?" said Esposito. "Who specifically was with you yesterday, if you don't mind me asking?"

"Aunt Barbara was with me. And Victoria stopped by for a minute, too. She's a guest of my mother's, you know—very nice person. Also, my mother and Sendrik came to see me. Mr. Wieland showed up while my stepfather was there, but he disappeared right away. I think he wanted to discuss something about my lessons, but probably noticed that I was really not well right then. And even later, when I had already fallen asleep, I think someone also looked in. I didn't really wake up, I just heard footsteps while half asleep, I think. I was so tired last night. Was it you who checked on me again?" she asked, turning to Sendrik.

He shook his head wordlessly.

"Did your teacher come by again, perhaps?" asked Esposito.

"Mr. Wieland? So late? No, that wasn't his style. Why

do you ask?"

He wanted to avoid answering her, but she wasn't prepared to put up with it.

"I may not be in very good health," she explained to the policeman, "but I'm not a toddler anymore. So please, out with it. I want to know what happened to Mr. Wieland. Did he really take his own life?"

"Do you doubt that?" Esposito asked her.

"Yes—no. That is, I just can't imagine that he would kill himself. But the idea of someone else plunging a knife into his stomach, of course, is even crazier." She shook her head.

"Now tell me what's going on," she demanded. "Why did you want to know if he visited me last night?"

Hesitantly, Esposito began to tell Juno about the photos they'd found on her teacher's cell phone.

"Photos of *me*?" she asked incredulously when he'd finished.

"Without any doubt," said the policeman. "Besides, in his suicide letter, his note, or whatever we might want to call this scrap of paper, Mr. Wieland wrote something about a sweetheart he had to protect. I guess that was about you as well, Juno."

She shook her head vigorously—which seemed to cause her pain. She groaned and refrained from pestering Esposito with further questions.

Instead, Sendrik took the floor. "Has Mr. Wieland ever behaved inappropriately toward you in any way?" he asked. "Has he approached you—"

"Never!" Juno interrupted him. "He's only ever been

my teacher. Super correct and above board. Sometimes strict, sometimes very kind, but he never got ... personal, if that's what you mean."

Esposito then ended the conversation, asking to see Juno's bedroom and also taking his leave at the same time. "For tonight, anyway," he said. "You'll hear from me again, of course, Dr. Leonhardt," he told Sendrik. "I think we can assume suicide, but we must still await the results of the autopsy."

After Pearl had returned to me and we were walking up the stairs to our room with Victoria, I felt tormented by more questions than ever before. Not the least of which was what had really happened in Diana's room the previous night.

"Did Mr. Wieland attack Diana last night?" I asked Pearl. "Was he stalking her, just as he'd secretly stalked her daughter? To photograph her? Was he possibly a man who harassed women in general? Or did Diana find out he was in love with her daughter and that he'd secretly invaded Juno's bedroom?"

"It's possible," Pearl said as she was hopping up from step to step. "But Diana could be insane just as easily. Maybe she herself played that recording of the howling wolves—to drive Dr. Bachmann to his death—and later Mr. Wieland as well? If she really has such a whatchamacallit ... such a split personality, then she probably has no idea what she's doing. The criminal part of her could have killed Dr. Bachmann and Mr.

Wieland. Maybe she just heard too many of those scary stories at the Wednesday Evening Club and went nuts."

"But you don't go crazy from a few horror stories, do you?" I objected anxiously. "Besides, Chris Wieland and this Dr. Bachmann seemed like two very sensible two-leggeds to me. I really didn't get the impression that either of them was prone to hallucinations or would even kill himself over a little wolf howling. None of this makes any sense!"

"I've no idea," Pearl grumbled. "I don't know what to think anymore. We practically witnessed a murder, and yet we don't even know who was actually the perpetrator and who was the victim. I never thought such a thing could be possible. Have you, maybe?"

24

Victoria crawled under the covers right after we'd returned to our guest suite.

First she tried to call Tim, but he wasn't available. Then she picked up a book, but after what felt like half an hour she had only turned three pages, so that didn't really help either. Her forehead was deeply wrinkled, and she kept staring out into the night through the room's large windows, seemingly sunk in thought.

At one point she looked down at me—I had placed myself on the bedside rug to her left—and said, "Look, Athos, we'll have a full moon soon."

She pointed in the direction of the windows. "I've never paid much attention to things like that before, but here in this castle you can't help noticing it."

She tried to devote herself to her book again, but with a similar lack of success. Finally Pearl decided that only cat cuddling could help to calm our human down. So she bravely sacrificed herself, jumping onto the bed and climbing into Victoria's lap.

The therapy seemed to work—as it so often does. Victoria's breathing became calmer, and the wrinkles on her forehead smoothed out a little. But the success was short-lived.

After Victoria had stroked Pearl's fur a few times, she suddenly rather rudely and precipitately lifted the midget up and set her aside.

Pearl emitted a severely offended meow, but that didn't make any difference.

Victoria swung her legs out of bed and hurried over to her closet. "I'm going to check on Diana again," she explained to us. "After all, she is my client, and this suicide...." Her face puckered. "It has really shaken her up, I think."

She looked at me, then at Pearl. "You two can come with me if you like. After all, you are my co-therapists, aren't you?" She tried a smile, but it only flitted across her lips very fleetingly.

Sleep, it seemed, had not yet found Diana either. She smelled strongly of alcohol, and even had difficulty staying upright on her feet when she met us at the door. When she caught sight of Victoria, she burst into tears without warning.

"Oh, it's all so terrible!" she howled.

"May I—may we—come in?" Victoria stammered, caught off guard by Diana's emotional outburst. She pointed to Pearl and me. "We'll keep you company for a bit, okay? And you can tell me what's bothering you."

Diana nodded vigorously, sniffled, and took a step to the side to let us in. But the next moment she had to lean on Victoria's arm to avoid losing her balance.

I could clearly see how our human sucked in a breath. Even her weak nose probably hadn't missed Diana's distinct alcohol smell.

We managed to escort the still-sobbing woman back

to her bed. Pearl lay down next to her, but for some reason Diana preferred to pat me on my head. I bravely held still, even though her caresses were not gentle. Rather than stroking me, she brought her hand down on my head in an amazingly rapid rhythm.

Victoria fortunately came to my rescue: she put her hand on Diana's arm and slowed her down. "Easy, dear, you're bashing his head in."

"What ... oh, I'm so sorry!"

A new fit of crying shook the poor woman. Then she blurted out the story that Pearl and I already knew—but which really disconcerted and astounded Victoria. Diana confessed to our assistant detective that she had killed the tutor—in self-defense, she kept affirming. She also described how Sendrik had faked Chris' suicide afterwards.

"He did it so I won't end up in the loony bin, do you understand, Vicky?" she cried. "I wouldn't survive that!"

Victoria had to take a few deep breaths until she regained her composure, but then she asked Diana several questions—similar to those Sendrik had already asked her.

But by this time the poor woman had dissolved in tears, and had nothing more to report beyond what she'd described of last night. She had been knocked down ... and then had regained consciousness with bloody hands, an equally sullied knife, and Wieland's corpse beside her.

"But there's something that won't let me rest," she

finally mumbled, after Victoria had done her best to calm her. "I don't know why Chris broke into my room and attacked me, but a day or two ago he was asking me some very strange questions—about Daniel Kirsch. It seemed to me that Chris was very concerned about Juno, and I found that touching at the time. But now Sendrik has told me that the police thought Chris was a peeping Tom, that he was supposed to have secretly photographed Juno..."

"Slow down, please," Victoria said. "What did Chris tell you about Daniel? What questions did he ask you?"

"Oh, I don't remember the exact words. My memory..." She shook her head.

"Alcohol kills brain cells," Pearl told me. "I heard that somewhere once. Diana really should stop drinking."

"The two-leggeds get hooked on the stuff," I replied. I, for my part, had learned this from Victoria. "They can hardly stop consuming it then, even if they want to."

"Poor humans," Pearl said compassionately. "They're really messed up. No animal would harm itself like this, poison itself with alcohol ... or even commit suicide, for that matter."

Diana tried to recall details of her conversation with Chris Wieland. "It seemed to me that he was concerned that Juno might marry Daniel," she finally told Victoria. "I guess he thought he was a gold digger, even an inheritance hunter. Yes, that's what it came down to."

"An inheritance hunter? But Juno would have to die for that to occur..."

Diana nodded with a deathly pale expression. "Yes. And I think Chris even suspected that Daniel wants to help things along, if you know what I mean. That's right—I remember now. I'm afraid I blocked it out, because at the time it sounded completely nonsensical. But now that Chris..."

"He implied that Daniel might hurt Juno?" Victoria interrupted her in amazement.

Diana nodded, barely perceptibly. "He didn't say it in so many words, but I think he suspected that Daniel was slowly poisoning her. So that she would grow weaker and weaker ... and then if she married him, he would only have to finish her off, and no one would be all that surprised if she succumbed to her lifelong illness."

New tears gathered in the corners of Diana's eyes.

Victoria handed her a fresh handkerchief. "This theory may not be as crazy as it sounds," she said gently. "People will do almost anything for money. And unfortunately, when someone has as bad a reputation as Daniel apparently does, there are often good reasons for it."

"Bad reputation? But a murderer, right away? Besides, people can change," Diana protested. "Daniel loves my daughter—haven't you seen how devoted he is to her? And anyway," she added, as if it were an afterthought, "he wouldn't inherit at all if Juno died. According to my late husband's will *I* would get everything in that case."

Victoria nodded slowly. She already knew that much from Sendrik.

At this point, she switched from therapist to full detective mode. Her curiosity was piqued; I could see it working behind her forehead.

"How did Chris come to ask you all these questions, and suspect Daniel?" she said more to herself than to Diana. "Was he possibly on a concrete trail—regarding Juno's illness?"

"I don't know," Diana sniffed.

Suddenly her voice took on a pleading tone, and she abruptly changed the subject.

"You have to keep everything I told you to yourself, Vicky! That I ... that I'm responsible for Chris' death. I was really just defending myself, I swear it. You mustn't tell anyone about this, or I'll be arrested for sure. Promise me?"

Victoria looked deeply conflicted. She hesitated for a moment, but finally gave her consent, nodding silently.

Diana had another question on her mind. She asked in a shaky voice: "Vicky ... am I really losing my mind? First these hallucinations, the memory lapses ... and now paranoia that my daughter might be in danger?"

And maybe committing murder, I added in my mind. I was far from convinced that Diana had not killed the tutor in cold blood.

When Victoria finally returned to her room with us, sleep was out of the question. First she paced up and down her living room like a caged lioness, then she threw herself onto the bed and stared at the ceiling.

Finally she addressed me, as she was so fond of doing. "What am I supposed to do now, Athos? Should I call the police, even though I gave Diana my word? She is my client, and I am bound by professional confidentiality ... but if she really has committed a murder, that would be quite another matter."

She tugged at the bedspread, then crossed her arms in front of her chest and pierced me with a fixed stare.

"In any case, Diana needs my help," she ruminated further. "And Juno should be examined again by a specialist. Sendrik is making an honest effort with her, but he's not a real expert. His ambit is new noses and similar embellishments, after all...."

25

The next morning Victoria had made up her mind.

"I have to take Sendrik into my confidence," she announced to us. "I can't make this decision alone, and I really don't know what else to do now. Sendrik may not be a fellow therapist, but he's still a doctor—and he already knows what Diana has done. Yes, he even helped her cover up Chris's death."

Right after breakfast, she set out with us to find Sendrik—and finally spotted him in a gazebo in the park, sitting at a table and working on his laptop. Apparently he still had to take care of his clinic business, even though he was on vacation.

Victoria got straight to the point and repeated to him the night's conversation she'd had with Diana. "She swore me to secrecy, but I can't keep that promise," she explained to Sendrik after she'd finished her report, "because after all, a man has died."

Sendrik flipped his laptop shut and ran his hands through his hair—leaving it completely disheveled. "Whatever you're going to do now, Victoria, please don't bring in the police, I'm begging you. What Diana confessed to you doesn't really change anything, after all. Wieland broke into her room in the middle of the night, and what do you think his intentions were? Probably the same as for my stepdaughter. I must reproach myself that I always thought the man was absolutely trustworthy, when he was in fact a psychopath! In the end he might have done something to Juno or my wife. With stalkers like that, it's only a matter of time, isn't it?"

"Not necessarily," Victoria objected, "but that's certainly not to minimize what he did."

"He was definitely no innocent, that is clear by now," Sendrik said.

"Those strange notes on his desk, about lycanthropy and not endangering his beloved—you didn't write those to cover up his death? After all, you faked his suicide."

"No I didn't! I wouldn't have thought of such nonsense. I merely took the body to his room and made his death look like suicide to protect my wife. That scribble is certainly not mine. Nor did I know the first thing about him being a peeping Tom who was secretly stalking my stepdaughter. I would have thrown him out long ago!"

Victoria nodded in understanding.

Sendrik continued in the same agitated tone: "My wife acted in self-defense; I don't doubt that for a second. But if you go to the police now with the story, and they find out that Diana has severe mental problems—delusions, panic attacks, memory lapses, and a drinking problem to boot—do you really think they'll believe a word of her version of events? In the end, they'd put her in a mental institution, you know that as well as I do. And there she would perish!"

He paused and looked pleadingly at Victoria. She

said nothing, but I could see how conflicted she was.

"*You'll* be able to help Diana as a therapist, I'm sure," Sendrik continued in an imploring tone. "She trusts you. And think of Juno, too, I beg you! She wouldn't be able to take it if she found out her mother has killed Chris. She was attached to the man, you know—"

"You're not saying that she reciprocated in any way the feelings he seems to have had for her, are you?" Victoria asked.

Sendrik scowled. "I hope not. I always thought she just had a crush on him, as can happen between a teenager and a charismatic teacher. That sort of thing is perfectly harmless, generally speaking."

"Generally, yes," Victoria repeated as if in a trance. The way she looked, though, it was as if the thoughts in her head were running amok.

"I caught Juno trying to flirt with him once or twice," Sendrik said. "But quite innocently, you see. I really didn't take it seriously. And he didn't seem to be encouraging it or responding to it in any way."

He lowered his head into his hands and moaned softly.

"Listen, Sendrik," Victoria said with compassion. "Let's leave the police out of this for now. I'm okay with that. But still, we can't just let this incident go. Diana needs help urgently. I'd like to consult a colleague who is a psychiatrist ... an expert in dissociative personality disorder. And whatever diagnosis he comes up with, I would definitely recommend that Diana checks into some kind of rehab clinic as well. Her alcohol addiction may be the main cause of her mental health problems."

"Diana's not going to consent to this," Sendrik replied. "To the clinic, I mean. She'll refuse to abandon Juno."

"She wouldn't be abandoning her! But she also has to take care of her own health."

"You don't have to explain that to me," Sendrik said, "but that's the way she'll see it."

"Then we'll organize a sober companion for her to stay at your house: a counselor who'll live here for a while and will help Diana through at least the first phase of withdrawal."

After a moment's thought, Victoria added, "I could even do that myself, if you'd like."

Something like a spark of hope flared in Sendrik's green eyes. Yet his expression was still somberly funereal.

"And as for Juno," Victoria continued, "my aforesaid psychiatric colleague could also subject her to some tests. Rare diseases whose cause cannot be determined can sometimes have a major psychosomatic component, you know. Maybe we'll find something; it certainly can't hurt to try. And as for your wife's, or rather Mr. Wieland's, suspicion that Daniel might be trying to harm Juno—"

"Dear God, did she tell you about that too? I really can't imagine it!" Sendrik interrupted her. "It's completely crazy. We can't be surrounded by criminals! Chris a stalker and Daniel a poisoner? Don't you think that maybe Chris only voiced this suspicion because he was jealous of Daniel?"

Victoria shrugged. "I can hardly get my head around everything, either," she said. "Daniel seems deeply devoted to Juno, and I really can't imagine him secretly poisoning her, but as I told you—unfortunately, you can't see inside people."

Sendrik groaned.

She went on, "Didn't you tell me that you would have noticed something like that? I mean, if someone really were intentionally harming Juno, poisoning her or whatever."

Sendrik was massaging his temples. "Yes ... that's what I thought, anyway. I could have sworn! But even so, I really don't know what to believe anymore." He glared at Victoria like a beaten puppy.

I licked his hand sympathetically, but in his state of tension he didn't even notice.

The morning sun was shining brilliantly above our heads, and the leaves of the gazebo where we were sitting rustled gently in the wind. The lush scent of flowers rose to my nostrils; in this world one would hardly have thought that any two-legged could conceive an evil thought. Not to mention stalking or poison attacks. But unfortunately appearances are deceptive.

"I would suggest that, apart from the psychiatric evaluation, we also have Juno examined by a specialist," Victoria told Sendrik. She looked extremely agitated, but she had kept her cool as a therapist despite everything. I was proud of her for that.

"I know an excellent chief physician in Klagenfurt," she said. "He wouldn't have to travel far to get here, and he would certainly be willing to take a thorough look at Juno. It can't do any harm, I think."

"Yes, all right, thank you. We'll do as you suggest," Sendrik said. "I trust you, Victoria. I—"

I have no idea what else he added, because at that moment a realization hit me—completely unexpectedly, but with full force. One that had nothing whatsoever to do with Juno's state of health ... or did it, perhaps?

26

"I got it, Pearl!" I shouted, jumping onto my paws as if bitten by a wild monkey.

"Phew, don't scare me like that!" she complained.

There was no time for an apology. "I just remembered where I've seen our castle ghost before! Come on, come with me!"

I sprinted off, back towards the castle. Sendrik made some comment to Victoria about what had gotten into me, but of course she had no answer. The two-leggeds stayed behind in the gazebo, but Pearl rushed after me.

"Athos, wait up!" she moaned, even though she had almost caught up with me. "Where are you going? What is it about the ghost? Now tell me!"

I squeezed through the large entrance door of the castle, which was fortunately only ajar and could thus be pried open, and entered the reception hall with Pearl. There I stopped, took a breath and began to look at the paintings on the walls.

"She's pictured in one of these ancestral portraits," I said breathlessly to Pearl, "I just can't remember which one. We'll have to search the house."

"That could take a while," she opined. "This place is huge!"

"Yeah, I get it. But don't you also want to know who she is—this girl who loves ghost stories but won't do any haunting herself? And who doesn't like dogs."

"As long as she likes cats..." Pearl replied in her inimitable way, but of course she was as curious as I was.

So we set out on a tour of the castle, starting on the ground floor. We ran down every corridor, looked into the rooms whose doors were ajar or which could be opened, and examined every wall and every oil painting that hung there.

The Messners must have practiced a real ancestor cult, because the walls were literally plastered with portraits of their long-dead family members.

"The family seems really old," Pearl gasped when we had already searched the ground floor and a good part of the first floor. "But they must also have been very strange people. Aside from the two-legged family members, they had their dogs painted, too, and even their horses. Yet I haven't seen a single cat in any of the paintings! What kind of weirdos *were* they?"

I did not get into that discussion. The answers that came to my mind would certainly not have pleased Pearl.

"Let's keep going!" I urged her instead.

"Why don't you try to remember *where* you saw this painting," she whined. "You have to think with your head, Athos, not with your paws! You can't be going senile already, can you?"

I let her vituperation wash over my back. After all, it was I who'd recognized the girl—because I had looked at the pictures on the walls in the first place. I am interested in the humans' art and history, while Pearl is more concerned with how tasty their food is, and how comfortable their furniture.

When I finally ended up discovering the portrait I was looking for on the wall of the very corridor where our guest suite was located, I must admit I felt a bit embarrassed.

"Look!" I exclaimed quickly, not wanting to give Pearl the opportunity for another pointed remark about my memory, or rather my incipient senility. "That's her!"

I came to a stop in front of a rather small-scale picture that showed a whole family. It was not a painting, in fact, but a photograph, even if it already looked very old. The composition seemed artificial and stiff, and the people depicted did not exactly leave a happy impression.

In the foreground, a stately woman sat in a reclining chair with a boy, perhaps two years old, on her knees. He looked as tortured as if he were in a dentist's chair and not in front of a photographer's camera. To the left and right of the woman stood an older man—presumably the spouse—and three other sons. On the far right, half hidden by one of the boys, a girl could be seen trying to smile, but still looking quite melancholy.

"Look," I prompted Pearl, "that's our castle ghost, isn't it?"

Pearl squinted her eyes and stared at the picture. "You're right; she looks just like our ghost."

Neither of us knew what to do with the realization. The elation that had overtaken me in the gazebo when the inspiration had come to me had fizzled out. I stood there like a wet poodle, wagging my tail in embarrassment.

At the bottom of the picture frame, right in the middle, a few words were written—which Pearl and I could not read, of course. Surely a clue as to who these people had been—their names maybe? And some information as to when they had lived?

"We need help," I said to Pearl. "A two-legged who can read these words to us ... and who might be able to use them to find out who the girl is. When and why she died so young. I'd really like to know why she's a ghost in this castle now, and not just because she wants to hear scary stories for all eternity, I presume."

"Maybe because she wants to kill people herself like in some of those horror novels?" Pearl said.

"Hmm," I replied. "Horrible idea." But a dog-hater was perhaps capable of anything.

"She could be driving the two-leggeds crazy," Pearl said. "Diana, for example. And she might have it in for Juno, who she'd like to have as a friend in the spirit realm. Can a ghost poison people, Athos?"

"How am I supposed to know that? You're the cat with the paranormal senses."

Pearl passed over my objection. "We definitely need to find out who this girl is," she said, "Or was, at least, when she was alive. Are we going to try Juno? She said she's sensed the ghost more than once."

"But she's never seen the girl," I objected.

"Maybe she'll still look familiar to her somehow, if we

bring her here to this picture."

That was a pretty optimistic assumption, but after all we had nothing to lose. We had to try.

We found Juno alone in her living room. It took her a long time to respond to Pearl's scratching at the door and my loud barking.

When she opened the door, she almost looked like a ghost herself; so skinny and so pale was she, with huge dark circles around her eyes.

She seemed very uncomfortable again today, but since it was Sunday—notwithstanding the fact that her teacher was dead—she had no classes.

She let us in and seemed very happy that we had come to visit her. She wanted to shuffle back to the sofa where she had been sitting—obvious from the blanket and the open book that lay on the seat—but I did my best to make her understand that she ought to come with us. I used the method that Victoria already knew how to interpret: insistent barking and running back and forth several times. To the door, then back to her, then to the door again. Pearl supported me with loud meowing and also meandered up and down between Juno and the door.

The girl was quick on the uptake: at first she asked us if we wanted to play, only to add with a wistful look that she was unfortunately not able to do so. But I didn't give up, and eventually she understood what we were about.

"You want me to come with you? You want to show me something?"

I confirmed this with even louder barking and wagged my tail like crazy. She grinned as if we were a conspiratorial group of adventurers.

"All right," she said, "but let's take it easy, please. I'm not so great on my feet, I'm afraid."

It took quite a while until we could eventually guide her from her room on the second floor to our corridor on the first, although there even was an elevator in the castle that we could use instead of the stairs. It had been installed especially for her sake, as she told us now. She talked to us, in the way that Victoria and so many other two-leggeds did—always assuming that we couldn't understand her language but would somehow comprehend what she was on about anyway.

Arriving at the old photograph in our hallway, I shifted back to barking, but instead of running back and forth, this time I bounced up and down in front of and as close as I could to the portrait of the girl and her family.

I think the little girl ultimately caught Juno's eye precisely because she stood so much on the edge in the picture, and not only in the spatial sense. She seemed to be an appendage of this family, belonging to it but not playing any significant role. Somehow it was sad, I thought—and Juno seemed to see it quite similarly.

In the end, she said exactly what Pearl and I were hoping to hear: "That girl looks kind of familiar. Do you think ... could she be our castle specter? The ghost in the library?" Juno's sixth sense was probably better than she had guessed.

She approached within inches of the photo and looked at it with narrowed eyes.

By the time she'd turned back to us, she had made a decision: "I'm going to look for this girl in our family archives," she said.

She glanced at the few words on the picture frame, unfortunately not reading them aloud, but seemingly memorizing them. After that, she shuffled slowly but determinedly back to the elevator.

27

We went together with Juno to the ground floor and directed our steps to the library.

One corner of the large room was apparently something like the Messner family archive; Juno headed straight for it and immediately began pulling some books off the shelves. Many of them were photo albums, which she first leafed through only superficially, while others were small handwritten volumes, probably diaries.

She grabbed a few of the books and settled down with them on the armchair closest to the shelves. Full of curiosity, like a young scientist, she plunged into her research. I settled down next to her and put my snout on her knee to give moral support. Pearl, on the other hand, suddenly ran over to the opposite corner of the room.

I heard her words—she was addressing the castle ghost.

For the life of me, I couldn't see anything of the ghostly girl today. I didn't even feel the usual coldness that emanated from her when I came near. And to my relief no book fell on my head.

Nevertheless, I listened closely to Pearl's words.

"Look," she said to the castle ghost, "Juno is researching your story now. We found your picture up in our corridor. That family portrait with the four boys and the parents ... that's you there, standing at the edge, isn't it?"

I did not hear the spirit's answer verbatim, but I had the impression that she was agreeing with Pearl. She seemed to like the fact that both the tiny one and now Juno too were interested in the story of her life.

Just as she had stood on the edge in the photo—lost, insignificant, only a secondary appendage of the family—so her entire short earthly existence seemed to have passed by. She told Pearl about it, lamenting the fact that no one had ever really cared for her.

Again I didn't hear her voice directly in my ears. But I could well feel her emotions, her melancholy and her loneliness. Paired with her joy over the fact that finally someone was interested in her.

Juno, meanwhile, spoke to me. She told me about the discoveries she was making in the books, even though her progress was slow.

At some point—I had almost dozed off while Pearl was still hanging out with the ghost girl—Juno suddenly let out an excited scream.

"Look, Athos, that's her, isn't it? The only photo that has her in it, apart from the picture hanging in the corridor upstairs. I've searched through everything now."

She had a leather-bound photo album lying open on her lap, its musty old smell tickling my nose. Euphorically, she tapped on a picture in which the whole family was again to be seen. Here only three of the brothers were present; presumably the youngest had not yet been born. But our girl—a few years younger than in the other photo on the first floor—was also standing here at the very edge.

"This is the same family as upstairs in the hallway," Juno explained to me. "Their photos fill this whole album, even though it's quite narrow."

She carefully leafed through the picture book and pointed to the pasted photos. "The Messners have always been very proud of their family history. They've never thrown away a diary or a photo album—that is, since the time when you could take photos at all. I don't even know when photography was invented," she added. "In the 1850s or something?"

"I don't know," I said, and sneezed, drooling a little on her pant leg. But luckily she didn't even notice, so excited was she about her find.

"Anton and Maria Messner," Juno read aloud, tapping the handwritten words under one of the photos. "I'm guessing that was the name of her parents. I think I've heard of Anton before. Wasn't he some kind of inventor? Hmm—anyway, he was the master of the castle in the first half of the twentieth century. My great-grandfather?"

I was distracted by Pearl, who was still talking to the ghost girl. I heard her say that I was honestly quite all right—for a dog.

"He really doesn't bite," she explained to the ghost. "But I can understand that you've had bad experiences with dogs. I feel the same way. Some of them"—she gave me an apologetic look—"truly are not very nice fellows. Loud, uncouth, and not nearly as cultured as my species."

A low growl escaped me. Her arrogance really went too far!

"Don't be so pompous, midget!" I barked. "You'd better ask her about Anton and Maria. I wonder if those were her parents' names."

Pearl complained briefly that I was calling her a midget again, but then she did as she was told.

The ghost answered the question in the affirmative.

The next moment I felt as if the spooky girl was approaching me and Juno. I still couldn't see her, but I felt a cold breeze brush the back of my neck again. It didn't seem quite as hostile as last time, though—or was it just me, the eternal optimist, imagining things? Was it possible that the ghost girl was beginning to trust me?

Juno raised her head to look at Pearl, who was approaching us together with the ghost, and then narrowed her eyes. She didn't say anything, though, and the next moment she had already put her nose back into the photo album she was working through. More photos of Anton and Maria appeared in it, as well as quite a few shots showing the sons of the family. You could literally watch them grow up.

There were pictures of birthday parties, of Christmas, and of the family against a school background, where the boys had apparently won certain awards. In any case, they usually looked very proudly into the camera.

Later the young men were depicted in military uniforms, on which badges and medals accumulated over time, then there followed new little boys—probably the grandchildren—and so on and so forth.

But no matter how much Juno rummaged, she couldn't find another picture that had our ghost girl in it. Of course she must have died young, but there was not a single photo from her childhood, either.

Meanwhile, Pearl continued the conversation with the ghost. "Will you tell me your name?" she asked.

This time it seemed to me that I could literally hear the answer. "Why do you want to know my name? I am a complete nobody. I always lived in the shadows ... until I suddenly died. And even then, hardly anyone shed a tear for me. I was only the daughter, a stupid girl, sickly and not a bit pretty. Just a burden, although my parents really didn't lack money—"

The fact that the girl had hardly been included in any of the family's pictures seemed to confirm her statement.

But Pearl did not give up. "*We are* interested in you," she said, accompanied by an exceedingly friendly meow. "Athos found your picture, and Juno is now looking for you in the old family records. That's great, isn't it?"

"Do you really think this is a smart idea?" I murmured to Pearl. "If she thinks Juno could be such a good friend to her, she might just want her to be with her all the more quickly. In the spirit realm, you know? She might get the idea of murdering Juno—if she's not already harming her. Maybe she's slowly sucking the life out of her, and no doctor in the world can tell. That could actually be the key to Juno's strange illness, after all!"

"Really, Athos," Pearl retorted. "Now you're definitely hallucinating! Get over the fact that she doesn't like dogs, and don't do her wrong. I think she's harmless; just a little lonely."

Such a rapid change of opinion was once again typical for a cat. Just a short while ago Pearl had thought the ghost capable of anything, but I didn't even try to draw her attention to this discrepancy.

The ghost girl's mood seemed to brighten the longer Juno pursued her research. She drew a little closer to us, and even seemed to temporarily overcome her aversion to me.

Juno flipped through more of the photo albums, but didn't find anything there either. In fact, there seemed to be almost no pictures of the girl.

At some point she paused, dug out her cell phone and called Francesco to ask him to bring some sandwiches to the library.

And she also generously thought of Pearl and me. "Oh, please bring some bites for Victoria's pets too, will you? They're both with me ... and they look pretty hungry."

"We look hungry?" I said to Pearl.

"I'm always hungry," she shot back. "And the castle chef is really talented." Her nose twitched in joyful anticipation.

After we'd fortified ourselves, and the cook had cleared the dishes again, Juno's eyes slid shut.

She just fell asleep in the fauteuil she was sitting in, curling up as Pearl liked to do when she took a nap.

I thought about checking on Victoria. After all, you had to take care of your human, didn't you?

But then I myself was overcome by fatigue and let my muzzle sink onto my paws. Just to close the eyes for a little while...

When I woke up again, Juno had moved on to the diaries. She was skimming the countless handwritten pages in the various volumes, and did not utter a word.

I could sense that the ghost girl was watching her expectantly and was very proud that Juno was so interested in her.

But then, after Juno had been reading the old volumes for what seemed like several hours, she flipped the book she was holding closed and cradled my head.

"This must have been a really strange family," she told me. "It seems that I've gotten to know the lives of all the male members of the family, as well as the mother. But about this girl ... there is hardly a word. In the old family chronicles it is only noted that Anton and Maria had a daughter who did not reach adulthood. Not a single sentence about her childhood, or about what she died of so early. I have not even found her name—one might think that she'd been a leper."

The temperature in the room dropped so abruptly that even Juno noticed it. She shivered and looked around, startled.

I knew where the coldness was coming from. The ghost girl, who had finally become a bit friendlier and more approachable, abruptly retreated to the other corner of the room and there seemed to have given herself over to her grief.

Pearl wanted to follow her, but received a threatening, "Leave me be! I want to be alone. I don't need anyone, I have my books and that's quite enough for me!" Then the phantom disappeared, literally vanishing into thin air.

28

The two-leggeds gathered in the dining room for dinner, but Victoria was not among them.

"What's wrong with her? Doesn't she have an appetite today?" Pearl asked me. She simply couldn't imagine that anyone was not as voracious as she.

"Victoria will come around," I said. "In the meantime, let's try our luck with Francesco; maybe he'll have some tasty snacks for us again." Unsurprisingly, Pearl immediately agreed to my suggestion.

The castle chef truly had a marvelous heart, because once again he fed us with pies and poultry, and Pearl even managed to scrounge up a portion of fish, albeit from a safe distance. By now she had even Francesco, the cat allergy sufferer, wrapped around her little paw.

Fish was Pearl's favorite food, and now she had apparently gotten that through to Francesco. Or maybe Victoria had given him a hint? Had she noticed that we spurned her dry food and secretly had sumptuous feasts in the castle kitchen?

I suspected it; after all, she would have had to assume that we were taking a fast otherwise, and that really wasn't our thing.

"Can't we take him home with us?" Pearl asked, smacking her lips with relish as we indulged ourselves in the hallway outside the kitchen.

"Who? The fish? It would go bad," I objected. "Besides, you can easily manage that portion, you little glutton!"

"I'm not a glutton, I'm a gourmet! And I don't mean the fish, silly—I meant the chef, of course. Maybe we could set Victoria up with him, and he'd have to cook for us every day."

"Do you have amnesia, midget? We've already set her up with Tim, haven't we?"

"She could have two guys even so—"

I gave it up and concentrated on my pie instead of having a discussion with a cat. It was pointless; I should really have known that by now.

Round as a ball and most satisfied, we returned to the dining room to finally join our human. Since we had spent almost the whole day in the library research-ing with Juno, we had neglected our two-legged owner a bit.

When we entered the dining room, one of the maids was serving dessert. But Victoria was still not there.

"Maybe she's left already?" Pearl suggested.

"I can't imagine that," I said. "She's not that fast an eater."

Nevertheless, we ran upstairs to the first floor to check on her. The door to our guest suite wasn't locked, but there was still no trace of Victoria.

Involuntarily my neck fur bristled, as if the spirit were once again brushing me with its eerie cold. But that was not the case. The ghost girl, whose name we still didn't know—and perhaps never would—pre-ferred to stay in the library. She had never haunted our guest suite. According to her own statement, haunting was not really her thing.

So was it a dark premonition that came over me? Did I suspect that something was wrong? Perhaps. Maybe dogs have a sixth sense just like cats, after all.

"Come on," I said to Pearl, "we have to find Victoria."

"Why is that?" The midget yawned. "She'll come around. I think a digestive nap would be in order right now."

I gave her a nudge with my nose. "No way ... I have a bad feeling about this. We need to find out where she is, and whether she's okay."

Reluctantly the pipsqueak followed me. We searched the first floor, then ran down to the ground floor. Again we looked in the dining room, but now only Barbara was sitting there, drinking a cup of coffee. The others had already left. We found them in the adjoining parlors, reading, having a drink, or chatting with each other. But Victoria was not among them.

She was not in the library, either. But the ghostly girl had returned there in the meantime. I felt her coldness in one of the cozy reading corners. Pearl ran up to her without hesitation and spoke to her as if she were a quadruped just like us. "Have you seen Victoria?"

"Who?" the girl replied impassively.

I could hear her loud and clear this time, as if Pearl were talking to me. Was I slowly becoming a ghost whisperer? Not an idea I liked—but I still hoped that the girl had met our human, or perhaps could help us find her.

"Our human," Pearl explained impatiently. "Has she been here tonight?"

"I'm not interested in people," came the reply. "I already told you. I was engrossed in one of my favorite books—Arthur Conan Doyle—but not the Sherlock Holmes stories that everyone reads. His spooky stories! They're just fantastic. Do you know them?"

I really didn't want to philosophize about ghost stories right now.

"Please," I interjected, "something might have happened to Victoria. Do you know where she is? Or maybe you could, well, float around the house? We can't get into all the rooms, but you ... you can walk through walls, can't you?"

"I've never tried that before," she replied. "Terrible idea."

I took a deep breath so as not to growl at her. After all, she was now talking to me—the dreadful dog. I guess that had to be valued as some sort of progress. But as it looked now, she would probably be of no help to us.

I turned and addressed Pearl. "Come on, let's search the rest of the house. We're not getting anywhere here."

We were already running toward the door again, when the ghost suddenly stood in our way. I felt as if I'd run into a wall of ice, and Pearl let out a startled meow.

"I saw your human," the spirit told us. "Earlier ... in the afternoon, when you were occupying my library."

"Occupying your library? We did the research for you ... and then you just took off."

"Don't argue," Pearl murmured to me.

I fell silent, even though it was truly not easy for me.

"I wandered around a bit and then stopped by the big writing room," the ghost said. "I like that room, too. There are some bookshelves there, and those wonderfully eerie paintings on the walls. Castle ruins in the moonlight—dark woods full of shadows and nocturnal creatures. And there she was, your Victoria. She was arguing, and it sounded pretty intense."

"She had a fight? With whom?" asked Pearl.

"Bastian. Strange guy ... but that's probably true of all the castle residents, even if they're not from my family."

"And what were they arguing about?" I asked.

But I received no answer. Even though she no longer threw books at me, I was still a member of the dog species—and therefore to be shunned. Besides, she seemed to have sunk into a melancholy musing over her family.

I caught a few snippets of thought. "All cranks ... not quite right in the head. Selfish and money-grubbing. The people in the books are always much nicer—"

"Please, dear spirit," Pearl said politely. "This argument—what was it about?"

"It was about Diana."

"Okay ... and what else, exactly?" Pearl drilled her further.

"I wouldn't know."

With that, she withdrew from us. I couldn't tell if she had just disappeared into another part of the library or if she'd vanished from the room altogether.

Pearl groaned. "She's really not easy to deal with."

I bared my teeth. "If this Bastian has done something to our human..."

"Maybe Victoria found something out," Pearl said. "About the murders. What if she was digging into him, interrogating him, and he saw her as a threat because of it. He could have—"

"It's because you insisted on making Victoria our helper," I accused her. "We put her in danger by doing so. And we didn't take good enough care of her; we left her alone for hours just to research the life story of that unfriendly ghost."

"We're not actually babysitting our two-legged, are we?" Pearl rejoined. "But come on, let's keep looking. We're bound to find her. If she hasn't already been—"

"Don't!" I interrupted her. "Don't even think that!"

We resumed our search, now with a new urgency.

I tried to follow Victoria's tracks through the house, pressing my nose to the floor and concentrating on catching her scent. The only problem was that her tracks, her smell ... they were pretty much everywhere in the castle. After all, she had been staying here for a few days and hadn't just been sitting around in her suite.

After our search on the ground floor and the upper floors had proved unsuccessful, we finally set our sights on the basement. It was raining outside, so she was probably not in the garden.

It really shouldn't have smelled of Victoria in the castle basement, because I was pretty sure she hadn't even entered it since we got here.

Nevertheless I picked up her scent trail there.

We dogs can smell the tiny flakes of skin that a human sheds. In addition we can scent the breath and sweat of the two-leggeds—which is sometimes truly no feast for the nose.

Victoria always smelled pleasant. She often used deodorants and perfumes, and of all things, the deodorant she had brought with her on this trip—a tart scent reminiscent of a coniferous forest—rose to my nose as I walked down the basement stairs with Pearl. It was only a very faint trace, but it was enough for me.

The entire castle seemed to have a massive basement, stretching over two floors, because the stairs led into the depths over two full turns. There were no vault windows, so it was pitch dark, and the air smelled fairly damp. The tripping footsteps of rodents could be heard in the distance, for whom this underground labyrinth must have been a true paradise.

Luckily the light switches were located where I could reach them, and you just had to push them, not turn them or anything else that wasn't dog-friendly.

I could only follow Victoria's scent trail, which was getting weaker and weaker, to the first basement level with some difficulty. I lost the scent several times, and Pearl also tried to use her own sense of smell, but my nose was the better one.

At the sound of the rodents that lived down here, I had to think of our friend Three-tooth, a stately rat that we had unfortunately not been able to bring with us to South Tyrol. Victoria—for all her love of animals—wasn't yet ready to accept rats as family friends.

Three-tooth's nose was outstanding—he probably could have tracked Victoria down here in no time, even if he preferred to use his olfactory prowess to sniff out food supplies rather than to rescue two-leggeds.

We searched through several storerooms, junk rooms, and pantries, until we finally reached a huge vault: the castle's wine cellar.

The moment I managed to open the door, I could smell Victoria intensely. But the scents of other castle residents also hit me. By now I knew most of them quite well. I could sniff out Bastian, Sendrik and Diana ... and Barbara? The avowed opponent of alcohol? What business did she have in the wine cellar?

At the foot of the steep staircase leading down into the vault lay our human.

29

My heart almost stopped, because at first glance I thought Victoria was dead.

But fortunately that was not the case; she was breathing, even though she was lying there quite twisted and bleeding from a head wound. I barked loudly, but when that didn't wake her up, I slapped my tongue right into her face. Frontally. That technique could wake the dead—and fortunately it didn't miss its effect this time either.

Victoria flinched, muttered, "Ugh, Athos, don't do that!" then snapped her eyes open.

She tried to get to her feet, but immediately fell back to the floor with a sharp scream, clutching her knee.

"Damn, that hurts!"

Pearl meowed compassionately and snuggled against her leg.

Victoria wrestled a tortured smile from herself. "I ... what happened, anyway?"

Only now did she seem to notice where we were. Her eyes darted over the countless wine racks and barrels that lined the walls, growing wide with astonishment.

"The wine cellar? But ... how did I get down here? And what time is it? Did I pass out?"

She felt her head, which had to hurt like hell, and tried to remember. "I was on my way downstairs to the ground floor, in the early afternoon ... I wanted to check on you two. You had flitted off so suddenly in the morning, as if stung by a tarantula. I thought you might have discovered something, my little four-pawed super-sniffers—"

She waved her hand. "I know I shouldn't humanize you like this, but occasionally you strike me as detectives on four paws, just like in books."

Her smile widened. "Crazy, isn't it? I really get the impression that you two are good at tracking down criminals, or that you even investigate outright, in your own way."

She made another attempt to get to her feet, stood swaying for a moment, but then a new pain seemed to shoot into her knee.

"She can't make it up the stairs by herself," I said to Pearl. "You stay with her, I'll get help!"

It hurt sometimes how little Victoria—or people in general—trusted us.

Pearl and I *were* detectives. And a lot more: emergency rescuers, comforters, bodyguards ... even if we had failed miserably in the latter role today.

I ran as fast as my paws could carry me, back to the ground floor and there in the entrance hall I started howling and barking and carrying on as if the end of the world were imminent.

After some time I managed to summon a few two-leggeds, even though they took far too long for my taste. Barking incessantly, I guided them to the cellar door, down the stairs and finally through the old underground maze in the direction of the wine cellar.

When Victoria heard our footsteps, she called out loudly to draw attention to herself: "I'm down here! In the wine cellar!"

It was no problem to free Victoria from her predicament with the help of the other two-leggeds.

Bastian and Sendrik carried her to the ground floor and into the nearest salon, where they put her on a comfortable couch. There she was bombarded with questions that Pearl and I were just as eager to ask her.

Barbara did not miss the opportunity to start a moral lecture right away.

"Were you trying to get a bottle of wine at such an early hour?" she asked Victoria in the tone of a strict head teacher. "Were you already so tipsy that you fell down the stairs? After all, the steps are wide and regular, how did you trip?"

I couldn't help but growl at the woman. She really was going too far.

"I didn't *want* to go to the wine cellar at all. I don't know how I got there," Victoria said, to my amazement. "All I can remember is that I was on my way from the first floor to the ground floor. I was looking for my pets."

"And that's when you fell down the stairs?" asked Juno. "But then how did you get into the basement?"

Juno had been the last to join the rescue team. When we'd already moved Victoria to the salon, she'd appeared, breathing heavily. She had probably—by her standards anyway—run to the elevator in a hurry after hearing my howl of alarm.

I felt guilty that I had startled her, but on the other hand I was quite proud that I had apparently been heard throughout the castle.

Victoria shook her head—only to groan abruptly.

"You need to hold still," Sendrik ordered her. "Your head wound needs stitches, and you may have suffered a concussion. And as for your knee—"

"I'll drive you to the hospital right away," Bastian interjected. "You'll be in the best hands there." He gave his brother a disparaging look.

Victoria took a deep breath and clenched her teeth until the pain had subsided somewhat. Then she said, "I didn't fall. I was pushed!"

Several of the castle's inhabitants simultaneously uttered an exclamation of indignation.

Then they all began talking in confusion. "Pushed? Are you sure? You mean you were attacked? By someone in the house? Were you able to see them? Are you sure you weren't drunk after all and just don't remember going into the basement?" The latter question from Barbara—how could it have been otherwise?

Victoria ignored them all. "We should call the police," she demanded instead. "Given what has already happened here at the castle, I think whoever did this to me wanted to shut me up for good. Maybe I've asked too many questions. Let's notify Mr. Esposito, and then I'll go to the hospital."

She looked around and addressed the maid, who had

also rushed into the room. "Do you have a driver's license? Would you be so kind as to drive me?"

The woman nodded in amazement.

Bastian raised his eyebrows. "You don't want me to drive you? What are you implying?"

"No offense," Victoria said, "but I don't trust anyone here at the castle anymore. It's not directed at you personally, Bastian. There is a murderer in our midst who will stop at nothing; I have come to believe that he is responsible for the disappearance of Dr. Bachmann, and perhaps for other crimes as well."

She glanced sideways at Juno, probably wondering if she was in danger too, but didn't say so openly. She also didn't mention the death of the tutor—which she now knew had not been suicide. But all these things preoccupied her just as they did Pearl and me, that much could be seen in her face. And she couldn't make any sense of it either.

Turning to the other two-leggeds, she added: "I therefore don't think it would be a good idea, in my present condition, to get into the car alone with anyone whom I would have to count among the suspects. I would be virtually defenseless—an easy victim."

"Now listen, Pearl," I said, turning to the pipsqueak, "this is all our fault! She was attacked because we made her sniff things out. She could have died."

For once, Pearl didn't have a cheeky answer ready. With a guilty expression, she snuggled up to Victoria, but said nothing.

"This murderer is clever," I mused to myself. "Another sudden departure, or a completely unmotivated suicide—that would have been noticeable at this point. But a domestic accident, a fall down the stairs ... if Victoria had broken her neck, possibly no one would have suspected foul play."

"But she survived," Pearl said. "The killer must have realized that—or do you think he thought she was already dead?"

"I can't imagine. It only takes a few steps to get from the stairs she fell down to the basement door. The attacker probably didn't go so far as to strangle her or beat her to death after the push hadn't killed her. The police would definitely have been able to determine that afterwards. Maybe he figured he'd at least intimidated her and physically knocked her out enough that she wouldn't keep hunting him. After all, she can barely move."

"But why did he carry her into the wine cellar?"

"I don't know; maybe to make it look like she was drinking on the sly, thus making sure her credibility is shot?"

Unfortunately, this was exactly the conclusion reached by Mr. Esposito, the policeman we'd already met.

Barbara had nagged a bit about whether it was really necessary to call the police—because of an 'unfortunate accident,' as she called it. But none of the other castle residents had objected, and Sendrik had finally picked up his cell phone and called Esposito.

The policeman first theorized that Victoria must

have suffered memory loss from the head wound, and that she had surely gone to the wine cellar herself—which, he added, was quite unusual behavior for a houseguest.

"You don't just help yourself to your hosts' wine collection," he muttered to himself, addressing no one in particular.

He also said, "I really can't imagine that anyone here in the castle would want to kill you, dear Dr. Adler. I have known the family for years, and they are all decent people."

"Decent or not, I certainly didn't imagine the attack," Victoria insisted. "I *was* pushed. So you're not going to do anything about this matter?"

"You're going to the hospital for now," the policeman said evasively, "you'll be safe there, anyway. And I ... will take care of everything else."

Which probably meant that he intended to do precisely nothing.

The maid Victoria had chosen to be her driver packed some clothes for her, and Victoria made her promise that she would take care of Pearl and me while our human was in the hospital.

"Don't worry about it," said the woman, who seemed very nice and obviously knew how to judge Pearl and me. "They both seem pretty independent and I don't doubt they can manage on their own for a day or two. Our Francesco will make sure they don't starve."

"I'm just going to get a checkup and I trust I can come back as early as tomorrow," Victoria said. "I hope I haven't broken anything."

Her knee still hurt like hell, she couldn't walk, but she had declined Sendrik's offer to at least take a look at the joint. She really didn't trust any of them anymore.

30

"We should take a closer look at Barbara," I said to Pearl after Victoria had left us. "I could smell her so distinctly in the wine cellar, and she really has no business down there, being such an opponent of alcoholic drinks."

"You think *she* attacked our human?" asked Pearl. "But why?"

"Because Victoria snooped around too much, asked too many questions? And we put her up to it! Besides, Barbara doesn't seem to like anyone except Juno. And even that could just be an act—maybe she wants to keep managing the million-dollar inheritance and is doing everything she can to keep Juno and Daniel from getting married. That's why she hired Dr. Bachmann, remember? Sendrik found out that she only brought the doctor into the house so that he would make the most hopeless prognosis possible for Juno, to scare Daniel off. It just shows how criminal this woman is. And if Dr. Bachmann possibly refused to do his job after Sendrik had exposed him, she simply killed him..."

"Let's take a look around her room," Pearl suggested.

Apparently my theory hadn't convinced her, and if I was completely honest I only half believed it myself.

But Chris Wieland's death did not fit into this picture. He had been killed by Diana, not by Barbara. Were there two depraved murderers at work in this haunted castle? Along with a peeping Tom, a grumpy ghost, and maybe a third potential killer, Daniel, who wanted to inherit Juno's fortune and wasn't aware that it wasn't possible because Diana was the next heir in line?

I couldn't imagine that with the best will in the world, even if everything looked that way; humans are known to be inclined to aggression, but it was a bit much to have taken place all at once.

Barbara occupied several rooms on the second floor. When she'd finally said goodbye to the others—as soon as Esposito and Victoria had left—and withdrew, we followed her up the stairs.

When she noticed us, she stopped and turned back.

"Well, you two, where are you going? You're all alone now, you poor things." She sounded quite friendly by her standards.

We continued to run after her, and when we reached the top of the second floor landing, Pearl snuggled against her legs. This tender gesture was designed to draw in every possible two-legged.

I supported her flattery by putting on my most trusting puppy-dog gaze, but I was under no illusions: it was Pearl's sweet-little-kitten act that finally gave us access to Barbara's realm. She lifted the midget up into her arms and suddenly smiled.

"Animals just instinctively know who to trust," she mused. "You're welcome to stay with me until your mistress comes back. That might take a while, though, I'm afraid. She seems to have been quite seriously injured to me."

"Because you pushed her down the stairs?" I asked her, despite her sudden friendly act.

But of course I received no answer, only a pat on the head.

If only I could make the two-leggeds give up this ridiculous habit, their constant maltreatment of my poor skull! They would certainly not have liked it if someone gave *them* one on the head at every opportunity.

Barbara's rooms were laid out magnificently. The furniture looked and smelled as if it were several hundred years old—which was often considered a valuable attribute by the two-leggeds. There were soft, silky carpets with fine patterns, and lots of oil paintings on the walls. Barbara apparently preferred still lifes and landscape paintings, because not a single one of the pictures showed a family member or in fact any human being at all.

She grabbed a thick book from one of the crammed shelves and settled down on a large green velvet sofa that occupied the best spot in the living room.

Pearl initially kept her company on the couch, but as Barbara became increasingly engrossed in her reading, she returned to join me on the floor.

I had already taken a look around the room and sniffed a little. A faint smell of alcohol could be detected, seeming to emanate from a closet, but apart from that I found nothing that I would have classed as suspicious in any way.

Pearl also pranced around the room, stuck her nose in the bookshelf, under the sofa, and finally disappeared inconspicuously into the bedroom.

I decided to hold my position in the living room; if I had followed Pearl, Barbara might have noticed. After all, I am not as small and imperceptible as the midget. And many people object to us dogs entering their bedrooms. Pure discrimination, but cats are often preferred.

When Pearl returned to me, she had nothing to report.

"Everything looks normal," she said. "There are certainly no murder weapons lying around."

We couldn't seriously have expected that, I guess.

We were almost ready to break off our mission of observing Barbara and slip out of the room when she put her book aside and abruptly stood up.

"Time for a nightcap," she told us, smiling expectantly and heading straight for the closet I had sniffed earlier.

When she opened the double doors, the smell of alcohol became stronger—and there was no mistaking where it was coming from.

In the upper part of the cabinet a house bar was concealed, equipped with many bottles and a few glasses. I could sniff out various aromas, detecting those drinks that people called wine, whiskey, cognac and vodka.

My former human, Professor Adler, had liked to have a nightcap in the evening, and Victoria also enjoyed a glass now and then. But Barbara Messner, the abstinence advocate par excellence, who had bawled Sendrik out just because he'd had a drink downstairs in the salon? Such a hypocrite!

Barbara stood for a moment contemplating the offerings, then reached for a bulbous bottle containing a golden-colored liquid. A sweet liqueur, I noted, as she uncapped the bottle and poured a generous amount into a glass.

"So that's why I could smell her in the wine cellar," I said to Pearl. "Not necessarily because she dragged Victoria there, but because she's been sneaking booze—while pretending to be a teetotaler in front of the others. We were completely on the wrong track!"

"She can still have attacked Victoria," Pearl suggested.

"Yeah, that's right," I admitted soberly. "We'll have to keep an eye on her."

"But we can't monitor all the occupants of the house," Pearl said in her professional detective's tone. "There are too many of them for that, and there's only two of us. We'd better concentrate on the two-leggeds who are probably going to be targeted next by the killer. Guard them, you know? Especially Juno, I think. She is about to inherit a lot of money, and Daniel seems to be after it. I think he needs it pretty badly."

"But Diana was also attacked—by Chris Wieland," I

pointed out.

"Yeah, but he's dead now," Pearl said. "Maybe he was even the victim."

I was panting, annoyed. So many theories, so many suspects ... and nowhere a clue as to who was really guilty. One day my poor head would explode!

"On the other hand, I don't like this Bastian guy at all," Pearl continued. "He's acting very suspiciously. The way he's always fawning over Diana ... he's crazy about her and wants to steal her away from his brother at any cost. And if she spurns him—" Pearl emitted a sound that resembled a person being strangled.

Really very striking; apparently, the midget was completely in her element, unlike me.

"Also, Bastian had a fight with Victoria, although we don't know why," she continued. "And he offered to drive her to the hospital earlier. Maybe to be able to complete his work and kill her?"

31

I didn't have an answer for Pearl; what could I have said?

Anyway, as far as Barbara's apartment went, we were done. I ran to the door of the room and barked to get her to let us out. I didn't necessarily want to open the door myself in her presence, even if I was able to. I didn't want her to end up getting the idea that Pearl and I were smarter and more capable than we looked, and then make us disappear into some basement hole, too.

It worked—Barbara seemed a little disappointed that we didn't want to stay with her, but on the other hand she was too absorbed with the sheer pleasure of drinking her liqueur to really care.

Pearl and I walked down to the ground floor. Diana was still sitting with Sendrik and Bastian in one of the lounges; the three of them were also enjoying a few drinks, but not actually talking to each other. Diana and Sendrik were each staring at their cell phone screens, while Bastian was reading the newspaper.

No sooner had we entered the room, however, than Diana said good night to the two men and made her way to her bedroom.

In the library we found Juno, who had retreated there with Daniel. The two seemed to be engaged in a highly emotional conversation that was clearly characterized by joy, not conflict.

"My mega-deal finally worked out, dear," Daniel reported excitedly, squeezing Juno's hands tightly and beaming so brightly that he seemed to light up the entire gloomy library.

Juno was happy for him. She asked him many leading questions, and from his answers Pearl and I were able to figure out what the deal in question was about: vintage cars. Apparently Daniel not only drove such a car, but he also sold them professionally. A foreign collector had now bought eight such vehicles from him all at once, and at a very good price.

"I can finally pay off my loan," Daniel said, as if in passing. "I'm going to cram the money down my banker's throat, that rapacious old pirate, and enjoy every second of it!"

"Did he give you any trouble?" asked Juno, suddenly serious. "Why didn't you tell me about it? I could have lent you the money in the meantime until your deal went through, couldn't I? Barbara keeps me on a pretty short leash, but over the years I've been able to put aside a nest egg, one she doesn't know about."

Daniel stroked her hair tenderly.

"Mooching off my fiancée?" he cried passionately. "Over my dead body!"

The two fell into each other's arms and began to kiss passionately.

"Do we believe his protestations?" I said, addressing Pearl. "Is he truly not after Juno's money?"

"Hmm," the tiny one opined. "Then he would also

have no reason to poison her slowly and murder her once she marries him."

"Maybe he's figured out by now that in the event of her death, Diana would get all the money," I said. "Then it would be wiser just to let Juno live and enjoy life with her fortune."

At these words, a new thought came to me: "Wait a minute," I cried, "he may have known about the will all along, and doesn't want to kill Juno at all. He's just making her so sick that he can lock her up at home or even send her off to a clinic after the wedding ... while he squanders her money, which she would have full access to, all without Barbara's interference."

"It's possible," Pearl said. "We'll have to keep an eye on Juno, anyway—and Diana, too. They're the two humans our murder case revolves around, don't you think?"

"But Diana could be either a victim or a murderer," I objected.

"Yeah, sure, but anyway, the killer—whoever he may be—is starting to get nervous. He attacked Victoria because she somehow got in his way, and he only very sloppily disguised it as an accident. Meanwhile he seems to be determined to do anything to achieve his plans. Whatever his goal is, I don't think he'll wait much longer. We have to stand guard, Athos! After all, we are the only proper detectives in this house. We can't count on the police."

I had to agree with her—at the same time, I was anything but satisfied with our performance in this case so far. We were very much in the dark.

"TV detectives always make it look so easy," I complained to Pearl.

I couldn't help but think of one of Tiny's favorite investigators, whose cases Victoria had been watching more frequently on her DVD player lately. He was a rumpled guy who wore an overcoat in all weathers and always smoked smelly cigars. He made a completely helpless and chaotic impression, yet asked the appropriate questions and thus brought down the perpetrator every time without exception. It was really impressive, even if I have to admit that I hadn't really warmed up to the man. His dog always had to stay in the car during the investigations, and the cranky inspector hadn't even managed to give the poor animal a name!

And as far as asking questions was concerned, even if Pearl and I had been able to independently interrogate witnesses and suspects—I would not even have known who among the castle's residents and guests I should interview and which questions to ask to lead us to the solution in this intricate case.

"We're just not TV detectives," Pearl said with grim determination. "We need to focus on our core competencies!"

She had certainly picked up that phrase from Victoria; the words sounded very psychological.

"And what is that supposed to mean?" I asked glumly.

"Well, we have to ask ourselves: what can we do better than any two-legged inspector? What advantages do we have because we walk on four paws, can't talk to people, and everyone thinks we're inferior? I would say at least two: no murderer sees us as potential witnesses who could be dangerous to him, or even as an obstacle if he should choose to strike. As a result we have often been able to overhear conversations that would never have been conducted in the presence of a two-legged detective. And we can stand guard without having to hide. And that's exactly what we should do now— we've already decided that, haven't we? Diana and Juno need to be protected."

32

I had no choice but to agree with the tiny one; I didn't have a better plan in any case.

But I didn't like her next idea one bit.

"As for tonight, I suggest I stand guard here with Juno and then escort her to her room," she said. "You keep watch over Diana in the meantime, okay?"

"You want us to split up?" I protested. "That's out of the question. It's far too dangerous for you. Any two-legged could wring your neck in no time."

"Pah!" said Pearl. "I'm not all that defenseless. Besides, why would anybody attack me? After all, we've just established that the killer doesn't see us as a threat."

"But if he attacks Juno and you try to intervene, he wouldn't hesitate to—"

I left the sentence unfinished. I didn't even want to imagine what a nefarious killer could do to the poor little pipsqueak. He would not have such an easy time with me; I knew how to defend myself!

"You patronize me the same way Barbara does poor Juno," Pearl complained. "You may mean well, but still..."

She extended her tiny claws as if to prove to me what a dangerous fighter she was.

Then she continued, "Besides, we don't have any other choice. There are only two of us, and we simply don't know who might actually get attacked. Maybe we're wrong, and neither Diana nor Juno is in danger. But we don't have a better idea, do we?"

Of course Pearl prevailed once again—as she usually did when we disagreed. I guess I really am just a big, overly good-natured softie.

I was about to leave the library to head to my guard post at Diana's, when an idea came to me regarding how I might still be able to protect Pearl, even though I would not be with her.

Juno and Daniel were still flirting and making out, and certainly were paying no attention to us anymore. So they didn't notice that I'd suddenly started barking, and for one purpose only: to summon the ghost girl who loved to hang out in the library and who understood Pearl's and my words, unlike the living two-leggeds.

"Hello, dear girl!" I called into the room.

How annoying that I still didn't know her name, but that couldn't be helped now. "Could you maybe keep an eye on my cat? You like cats, don't you? Much better than dogs. I'm running upstairs to Diana now, but if anything happens down here, if Pearl—or Juno—is in danger, would you please come floating upstairs and alert me?"

I could sense that the ghost girl was near me, but she gave me no answer. If anything, I heard a cold rejection, along the lines of, "*I have no interest in your affairs.*"

"She may still be hoping to get a co-spirit when Juno

is murdered," Pearl pointed out.

She gave me a tender push with her miniature snout. "It'll be all right, partner," she said lightly.

I grumbled to myself, then got up onto my paws and left the library without turning around again. I really did not have a good feeling about this.

Upstairs on the second floor, I scratched at Diana's door and barked to get her attention.

Fortunately I didn't have to wait long for her to open up for me.

"Athos? Oh, you poor thing, you're all alone without your mistress. Come on in!"

She glanced out into the hallway, probably to look for Pearl, but then closed the door behind me and returned to her bed. She had apparently not yet been sleeping. The bedside lamps were burning, and on the bed was one of those electronic devices that some people like to use for reading.

I settled down on the bedside rug while Diana returned to her book.

Then ... well, nothing happened at first.

I had to fight against fatigue. There had been no time for regular naps today, but at the same time I was racking my brains over whether Pearl and I would ever be able to solve this strange case here in the castle.

What if Victoria returned from the hospital in a few days and then simply went home with us—intimidated by the attempt on her life?

Would another crime happen here in the castle without us being able to do anything about it? Or had the murderer already achieved what he wanted, no matter how much Pearl and I were in the dark about his motives? And was said murderer in fact lying next to me in bed and peacefully reading a book?

I must confess to my shame that I had fallen asleep when suddenly there was a knock at the door.

I got up onto my paws with a startled yelp and ran over. There I pushed down the handle before I could stop myself. I half expected to see the ghost at the door, coming to report that something had happened to Pearl, but ghosts hardly knock on doors.

As soon as I'd opened it, I smelled—and saw—Bastian Leonhardt. He looked down at me in amazement, then over at Diana, who was just swinging her legs out of bed.

"Did you get yourself a new butler?" he asked in a joking tone, pointing at me. "A truly original way to receive visitors, I must say."

"Hello, Bastian," Diana greeted him wanly. "What time is it?"

When I turned to her, I saw her yawning. And from the way she looked, her enthusiasm over her nocturnal visitor seemed to be quite limited. She had probably also been asleep already, although her bedside lamps were still burning and the e-reader was lying next to one of them, ready to hand.

Bastian stepped into the room and closed the door behind him.

I could feel my fur start to bristle. Had the time arrived? Was *he* the murderer, coming to finish Diana off for good? Or would he try to hit on her again ... whereupon she would kill him, just as she had already done with Chris Wieland?

It was really no good for a dog to ask so many questions. We are clearly not made for this, and my head was already throbbing badly from the constant brooding and doubting.

I took up position on the bedside rug again, determined not to fall asleep this time.

Diana crawled back under the covers, peering longingly over at her e-reader, while Bastian started another courtship ritual. He settled down on the edge of the bed and once more tried to explain to Diana why she would be so much better off with him as her husband than with Sendrik.

I wondered seriously why she didn't just throw him out. She even smiled at some of his compliments, and his assurances of how much he adored her. Was she not as averse to him as I had assumed?

Did anyone actually understand these two-leggeds?

Bastian stayed for a long time, talking without cease, while I had to fight fatigue yet again. Besides, it was damn warm in the room.

Should I move to the terrace? What was happening next to me on the bed really didn't look that dangerous. Neither of the two two-leggeds seemed to have it in mind to murder the other.

I changed my reclining position several times so as not to doze off, until I suddenly thought I heard a strange noise—or had I felt it, rather?

33

It seemed as if the ground beneath me was vibrating barely perceptibly, as was often the case with the weak earthquakes that passed the two-leggeds completely by.

I left the bedside rug and dropped a few steps further onto the bare parquet floor, which didn't muffle the sound, the soft trembling, quite so much.

Indeed, I had not imagined it. But what I was hearing was not an earthquake; rather it was repeated dull knocking noises, accompanied by a faint vibration. Just as if something was falling to the ground beneath me. Not just once, but again and again. Plop ... plop....

My brain was working only slowly. As I've said, my skull was humming, I was tired ... but then a thought flashed through my mind that made me perk up suddenly. Diana's room was diagonally above the library—was Pearl still there with Juno? Or had the two of them long since moved into Juno's bedroom?

The rumbling continued. Diana and Bastian didn't notice a thing, but I certainly wasn't imagining the noise and the vibrations. What was going on down there?

I debated for a moment whether I should leave Diana and Bastian alone—and finally decided in favor of it. They surely wouldn't be at each other's throats while I briefly checked on things among the bookshelves. And if someone else wanted to kill Diana, I doubted he'd try it in Bastian's presence.

So I ran to the door, opened it, and stormed out into the hallway. I chased the sounds down the stairs, imagining that I could still hear the little plopping noises—even though my own footsteps now drowned them out for the most part.

Finally I reached the library, opened it for myself—and was nearly scared half to death as I rushed into the room.

Pearl was clambering about on the bookshelves like a wild-eyed little monkey, knocking books off the shelves at random.

"There you are at last, Athos!" she called breathlessly when she caught sight of me. "You've got to save Juno! He injected her with something, a sleeping drug, I think—and now—oh, no, look! He wants to drag her out onto the terrace. Surely he's going to push her into the abyss!"

The whole room seemed to spin in front of me. Everything was happening so fast, and my heart was hammering in my chest.

I caught sight of Sendrik, who was holding his stepdaughter in his arms and heading for the terrace doors with her. He registered that I had appeared, but paid me no further attention.

Juno seemed to be fast asleep, and Sendrik was carrying her—not gently like a loving father, but like someone dragging an unwanted burden—one that he planned to get rid of as quickly as possible.

My thought was immediately confirmed. Sendrik let Juno drop onto the floor next to him and yanked open the terrace doors. She groaned, but did not come to.

Pearl landed next to me with a giant leap.

"He injected her with the contents of the two vials you see over there on the table," she cried, her words almost tumbling over each other. "He came right after Daniel left. Juno wanted to read some more, and Sendrik made her believe that he was going to inject her with some tonic that would do her good. She let him do it, but then she quickly became very tired. And I noticed that the vials look exactly the same as the ones Sendrik used with Diana on the day we arrived here at the castle."

"The tranquilizers, you mean?" I exclaimed.

"Yes! I tried to get the ghost girl to intervene. But she wouldn't. That's why I was throwing the books off the shelves—I swore to her that if she didn't help Juno, I'd devastate her whole beloved library. And I hoped that the noise would be heard in the castle! I can't yell as loud as you," she added, almost meekly.

"I heard you," I replied quickly.

But now was really not the time for a long conversation. Sendrik had just opened the terrace doors and was now preparing to lift Juno up again.

"Quick, Athos! Do something!" Pearl squeaked. "You've got to stop him—he's going to kill her!"

I ran. Barking wildly, I charged toward Sendrik, who had just stepped out onto the terrace with Juno.

He cursed when he heard me and whirled around,

holding Juno's limp body in front of him so that it would serve as a shield. I tried to snap at him from the side, but he was very nimble on his feet. He turned so that I always had Juno in front of me. If I bit furiously and wildly, I would only hurt her.

"Get out of here, you stupid mutt!" he cried—but I noticed that he hardly raised his voice at all.

Noise! That was the solution! I had to alert the other inhabitants of the castle. I started to howl and bark wildly, but at the same moment I realized that there would not be enough time.

Sendrik had already worked his way backwards, step by step, toward the terrace railing. It was chest-high here, but he was strong enough to lift such a skinny and lightweight person as Juno right over it. And behind the glass wall, the ridge was much narrower here than it was just a few feet away, under Diana's balcony. The library terrace was perched almost directly above the waterfall.

If Juno were hurled into the depths here, she would stand no chance of surviving.

I barked like crazy, bared my teeth and kept trying to grab Sendrik or at least push him away from the railing.

I heard Pearl behind me start knocking books off the shelves again. The ever more rapid fall of more and more volumes sounded like a roll of thunder. Also, Pearl was screaming at the ghost, "Come on, help her already! *Pleeeease!*"

I heard a tearing—leaves being torn out of books.

And then Pearl's voice again. It sounded by now as fierce as that of an actual tigress. "Come on, spirit, help Juno!"

Rip! Rip! More sheets were torn out.

I snapped at Sendrik's leg, but he quickly pulled it away. Again he spun Juno's limp body around so that I almost drove my teeth into her legs instead of his. The next moment he lashed out and kicked me. Pain shot through my body. My anger grew.

Where were all of the castle's residents? Were they all fast asleep? And had they heard too much wolf howling around the place lately—plus my own barking in the house—to pay much attention to my wild alarm cries now?

The book murdering behind me continued with un-diminished fervor. Volumes fell to the floor, others were torn to pieces. The pipsqueak was raging like a berserker.

Finally—at last!—just at the moment when Sendrik had aimed a new kick at me to keep me at a distance, and at the same time lifted Juno up to finally throw her over the railing and into the depths, it happened.

I felt a blast of ice-cold air that swept over me like an Arctic gale and made me yelp.

In the next moment, the ghost girl manifested her-self—right in front of Sendrik!

For the first time I could see her clearly, a still very childlike creature with long disheveled hair that could hardly have frightened a grown man when she'd been alive.

But now, appearing as she had out of nowhere, flailing her arms wildly and screaming at Sendrik—she scared the hell out of him.

He let out a scream—and dropped Juno. She landed on the terrace at his feet, not in the abyss. But it really wouldn't have taken much.

I seized the moment.

34

I would like to emphasize at this point that under normal circumstances I am an extremely peace-loving dog. But now I didn't miss the chance to open my muzzle wide, pull back my lips, and sink my teeth into Sendrik's thigh with a wild roar.

I was satisfied as I heard his shrill cry of pain, felt his warm blood spurting in my face, and yanked him to the ground.

He slapped his hands at me and tried to crawl back toward Juno, who was lying on the ground just half a dog's length away from us.

But when I increased my bite pressure, he abandoned his plan. He fought me for a few more moments, but at last finally gave in. I pushed him against the glass railing, where he remained huddled and pressing his hands on his bleeding leg. Threatening, growling, I built myself up between him and Juno, so that he could no longer be a danger to her.

"If you try to escape," I hissed at him, "I'll bite your other leg, too."

But he was no longer able to stand, let alone try to run.

The ghost girl had disappeared again immediately after her short, immensely effective appearance, and returned to her bookshelves, furious. Probably she was crying there now over the destroyed volumes that she loved so much.

She would probably never try to become a friend of the living again; she'd had too many bad experiences with the two-leggeds in the castle. And after what Pearl had done to her books, cats were now probably on the enemy list as well.

Pearl appeared next to me. I could hear her little heart hammering in her chest. Her baby blue eyes were fixed and wide with shock.

She ran to Juno, pressed herself to her head and licked her face, but in the end failed to wake her up. The anesthetic Sendrik had given her must have been strong enough to knock out an elephant. Besides, the poor girl might have broken a bone or two in her fall. But she was alive, and she was out of danger. Her step-father would never be able to hurt her again; that was all that mattered.

Finally, the first of the two-leggeds appeared in the library—no doubt attracted by my barking. But they had really taken their time.

Soon Pearl and I—along with my prisoner and the poor, unconscious Juno—were surrounded by two maids, Barbara, and at last by Bastian and Diana.

Sendrik tried to convince the others that I had viciously attacked him for no reason and that he'd only wanted to defend Juno, but Diana was fortunately quick-witted enough not to believe his lies.

She tried to wake her daughter, panicked when she failed to do so, but fortunately also saw that I had done nothing to the girl. Juno may have suffered a few bruises and at worst a fracture when she'd fallen, but she had no open wounds that could have come from me.

One of the maids then pointed out the syringe and the two empty vials of anesthetic lying on one of the small tables in the library.

"Looks like Juno was given this stuff," she opined.

Diana ran over to the little table and reached for the two tiny bottles. Of course she immediately recognized the medicine that Sendrik had surely given her several times before.

With an angry look, she came back to the terrace and hissed at her husband, "You injected Juno with *this*? It's way too high a dose. Were you trying to kill her? And why are you even out here on the terrace?"

At the same time I gave up my growling, sat down on my hindquarters like a good dog and put only one front paw on Sendrik's leg—the intact one. With this I wanted to show the inhabitants of the house that I was not a killer dog gone wild, but that I had attacked this monster for good reason.

Sendrik had no excuse for the narcotic overdose. He tried to pull himself up but his pain was too great.

"Will someone actually call an ambulance?" he growled, then dropped his head into his hands and suddenly burst into tears.

"Apart from this stupid mutt ... th-there was a damn ghost!" he suddenly stammered. "I saw her before me, as I see you now! God help me!"

The others looked at him as if he had lost his mind.

After calling an ambulance, the castle residents also immediately alerted the police—and Esposito appeared shortly after the paramedics from the ambulance service had doctored Sendrik and injected Juno with an antidote that allowed her to regain consciousness.

Both stepfather and stepdaughter, perpetrator and victim, were taken to the hospital, and Esposito promised to open a police investigation into Sendrik.

35

On Wednesday evening, the police inspector finally returned to the castle to give us a full report on what his team had found out in the meantime.

I must admit that I felt a bit crestfallen about this turn of events, that at the end Esposito should stand in front of us and present the resolution of the case ... *our* case. But Pearl comforted me with the knowledge that we had saved Juno and thus were the real heroes of the story.

"Core competencies—remember?" she said, impressing me once again with her unwavering self-confidence. "We're not human, so we can't interrogate suspects, and we can't present great resolutions at the end of the investigation like TV detectives do. But no policeman in this world could have called in a ghost to help, or bitten the murderer in the leg at the end. Right?"

I couldn't disagree with her. Besides, Esposito was actually quite a sympathetic cop. At least he didn't wear a rumpled coat, or smoke smelly cigars—and he didn't address me as 'dog,' but knew my name. Pearl's too, of course. In the report he gave to the castle occupants, he also mentioned us several times with praise.

So, at least on second glance, the world was perfectly fine.

I was also very pleased that, when he appeared at the

castle that Wednesday evening, he brought Victoria with him. She had already been allowed to leave the hospital again, and Esposito had kindly picked her up on his way here.

Her right leg was stuck in a complicated frame, and she hobbled into the house. Apparently her knee had been seriously injured, but she assured Diana, who welcomed her with a hug, that she would be 'as good as new' in six to eight weeks. Pearl and I greeted her with a few wet kisses, which for once she bravely endured.

Then we all gathered in the library, where Esposito began his *denouement.* I knew the word from the television detective stories and was quite proud of myself for it. It sounded so delightfully clever, so expert, and denoted the resolution of a criminal case. Much better than *core competency*, Pearl's new favorite phrase.

"It's really just a coincidence that I've come to you on a Wednesday evening," Esposito began as he let his gaze wander over the bookshelves—which had been tidied up in the meantime. "After all, I know all about your traditional Wednesday Evening Club; I was even allowed to attend once as a guest during Alexander Messner's time. I would also have come on a Thursday or Friday if we had concluded the investigation on that day, but I find it somehow fitting—perhaps ironic—that we are here on a Wednesday. Because what I have to report to you is a truly terrifying story ... and supposedly there was even a ghost in it."

"You seriously think my brother saw a ghost?" Bastian objected.

He was sitting next to Diana on the sofa, and had tried to put his arm around her shoulders. However she had moved away from him; she was probably not in the mood for romance after her husband had turned out to be a ruthless killer.

Esposito nodded slowly. "At any rate, that's what he kept affirming during the interrogations. He wouldn't budge from that assertion, even if he otherwise tried to give us all kinds of possible versions of events."

"That's crazy," Barbara said.

Juno, on the other hand, exclaimed, "That must have been our library ghost—oh, how I wish I could have seen her too!"

"Albeit under different circumstances," Daniel added.

"What? Yes ... sure. I never want to get that close to the spirit realm again, almost ending up there myself. I've had enough of near-death experiences for the rest of my life!" Juno laughed harshly.

It was obvious that the shock of that night was still in her bones, even if she looked so much healthier since her stepfather could no longer poison her.

"You know," Esposito said, addressing no one in particular, "I've never encountered a ghost myself, but I have no problem believing in such a possibility. Up here in the mountains you hear many a strange story that would sound ridiculous down in the cities. When I was a child, my grandmother, who grew up around here, told me many old tales about ghosts, nature beings, gnomes..."

He smiled, probably at the memory of his grand-mother. She herself had to have been in the realm of the spirits, because Esposito was no longer a young man.

I asked myself involuntarily, if as a dog—or a cat—one also entered the hereafter when one died. Proba-bly, because our two-legged friends would certainly be totally lost there if they had to get along without us.

Esposito returned to his denouement. "At first, Dr. Leonhardt came up with all kinds of excuses during our interrogation. But my team and I took another very thorough look at the events of the last few days here at the castle. I am honestly not proud of the fact that I didn't recognize the seriousness of the situation, or the danger you two—dear Juno and Diana—have been in."

"You really don't have to blame yourself," Diana said quickly. "Who could have guessed that my husband would be such a..."

Her voice died, and tears formed in the corners of her eyes. She tried to quickly wipe them away.

Esposito nodded at her gratefully. "In our investiga-tion we found, first, that Dr. Bachmann had not re-turned to his practice, and as most of you already know we found his body in the ravine below the castle. Dr. Leonhardt finally confessed that he killed the doc-tor because Bachmann was on to him."

Diana turned to our human, explaining: "Dr. Bach-mann must have found out, or at least suspected, that

Sendrik was slowly poisoning my daughter." Victoria had probably not yet heard this information because of her hospitalization. "That's why the man had to die—and poor Chris, too," Diana added breathlessly. "He even witnessed Sendrik try to kill Juno, didn't he?"

"That's right," Esposito confirmed. "The confession was very difficult to extract from your husband. It was only at the very end, this morning in fact, that we were able to persuade him that he could possibly hope for mitigating circumstances if he willingly confessed to us all the details of his deeds. Which is not to say that he will get off with a lenient sentence," he quickly added. "You don't have to worry about that. He can never be a danger to you again."

Victoria took the floor: "I'm sorry, but I don't even understand what Sendrik was actually trying to accomplish with all this madness. Had he decided to kill Juno so that Diana could inherit Alexander Messner's fortune?"

"That's right," Diana said grimly before Esposito could offer a response.

However, he took it upon himself to provide Victoria with a more detailed explanation. "Juno was supposed to die, but Dr. Leonhardt wanted to make it look like a prolonged illness with a fatal outcome. Direct murder probably seemed too risky to him at that stage. And your health has been rather poor from childhood, hasn't it?" he asked Juno. "So all he had to do was ... well, help things along a bit. No problem for a doctor."

She nodded. "He shamelessly exploited my weakness," she added tonelessly.

"I'm so sorry," Esposito murmured. "I don't even want to imagine what you must have been going through."

"And he only married me in the first place to get Juno's money," Diana addressed Victoria. "That pig!" Her voice quivered with anger.

Esposito cleared his throat. "That's the way it was, I'm afraid. He earned fairly decent money with his practice, but it did not compare to your family fortune. And human greed can be immeasurable, unfortunately. So shortly after your marriage, he began sabotaging Juno's health. Slowly at first, so it wouldn't be noticed, but lately on a more massive scale. He used various drugs and low-dose poisons that could not be detected later in an autopsy, but which would have had a lethal effect over a longer period of time. Only when the events here in the castle came to a head—first through the suspicions of Dr. Bachmann, then by Mr. Wieland almost witnessing an attempted murder ... and finally when you, Dr. Adler, suggested to call in a new wave of experts ... our murderer became impatient and therefore careless. He was afraid that his beautiful, meticulously-pursued plan would go up in smoke. And that could not be allowed to happen."

"That's why he finally drugged me and tried to throw me off the terrace," Juno said tonelessly.

Again Esposito nodded. "It was his second such attempt, even if you hadn't noticed. The first time, Chris Wieland probably entered your room just as your stepfather was about to put you under. If your teacher hadn't shown up, Dr. Leonhardt would have thrown you off the terrace of your bedroom into the abyss as soon as you were anesthetized and defenseless. Forgive me for this remark, but after all, this castle is ideally placed for a murderer, that has to be said."

36

Esposito pulled out a handkerchief and wiped the sweat from his forehead.

Then he continued: "Wieland saw that Dr. Leonhardt was about to inject you with an anesthetic, for which there was absolutely no medical reason. You weren't in a panic, or anything like that. And he had probably suspected for some time that someone was tampering with your already poor state of health. At first he left the room startled, perhaps still unsure whether what he had seen could actually be true. But that same night, he and your stepfather had a confrontation, and Wieland threatened that he would call the police. That's why he had to die."

"I didn't even realize Sendrik was drugging me," Juno said. "I mean, he was always injecting me with some kind of medication, so I no longer paid attention to what it was anymore. I was always being given so many different drugs ... and I blindly trusted my stepfather. It also happened that I got tired and suddenly fell asleep very often, without any anesthetic at all."

"Oh, my poor darling!" Diana sighed, still fighting back tears, "what have I done to you by marrying him! This monster that I brought into our house!"

"You couldn't have known, Mom," Juno said. "And besides, he had it in for you just as much."

"That's right," Esposito intervened, "you, Diana, were

to be driven mad. Two deaths in the family within a very short period of time would have been too suspicious; that's why Juno should succumb to her numerous illnesses first, and you would slowly but surely lose your mind. Your husband confessed to us all the abominations he had devised to make you think you were going mad."

"The howling of wolves, the fluttering of bats in my room, blood on my pillow, ghostly lights in the night, vampires drawing my blood ... it was all just him, of course," Diana enumerated bitterly. "With the help of a cell phone and a few medical tricks, nothing more. I drank so much alcohol because I was so scared, and that just made it all the easier to fool me."

Apparently, Esposito had previously described to Diana in either a face-to-face conversation or phone call some of the artifices her husband had used to drive her to the brink of insanity.

"Exactly," he said now. "And everything always went hand in hand with the current theme at the Wednesday Evening Club."

"I really thought I was only hallucinating because of those stories," Diana continued again. "And then he also made sure I got a quick look at Dr. Bachmann's body before he made it disappear into the ravine, never to be seen again. He lured me out onto the terrace with a hideous wolf howl, and out there I saw the dead man—and immediately afterwards he threw him into the abyss. I really thought I was going crazy!"

"And he also instigated the drinking you were doing

to combat your anxiety," Esposito said.

"That's correct," Diana said. "In the beginning, he would say things like: '*Come on, have a glass so you can relax.*' Then later, when I was already addicted, he would pretend to be concerned about my increasing alcohol consumption. But he never actually stopped me from drinking."

"So you were supposed to lose your mind," said Victoria, still looking as if she'd been struck by lightning, and visibly struggling to process all these ghastly acts of Diana's husband. "Then he could have put you in a clinic, or locked you up at home, and maybe even driven you to suicide after some time—or faked such an act, anyway, just so he could end up enjoying Alexander Messner's vast fortune all by himself. A plot straight out of a Victorian Gothic novel." She shook her head in disgust. "What a monster!"

"You can say that again," Diana agreed.

Esposito continued: "Moreover, Dr. Leonhardt very cleverly engineered the tutor's death, because he had become a dangerous witness, and used it as a new weapon in his arsenal, as it were. When it came to the confrontation in Wieland's room, he stabbed the teacher in cold blood before he could alert us. Then, a little later that night he took the body to his own room, and when you had fallen asleep, Diana, he crept into your bedroom, knocked you unconscious, and placed the body in front of your bed."

"And he smeared me with the dead man's blood," Diana explained to the others present. "He tried to convince me that *I* had killed poor Mr. Wieland! And I believed him."

"It would have given him the perfect leverage against you in the future," Esposito said. "If you had ever pushed for a divorce, or somehow rebelled against him because he wanted to put you in a clinic, for example ... he would have merely blackmailed you with it: *I'm going to tell everybody that you're a murderer if you disobey me. And then you'll end up in prison.* Something like that, I imagine."

"Incredible," Victoria muttered to herself. "What criminal creativity this man has unleashed!"

"That's true," Esposito said. "And he was far from finished with his machinations. Late in the night, when everyone was asleep, he moved Mr. Wieland's body back to his room, scribbled some insane notes on a piece of paper he placed on the desk ... oh, and even before that he had already taken those photos of Juno with the tutors phone. I almost forgot to mention it. Immediately after killing Mr. Wieland, he grabbed his cell phone, crept into Juno's room and secretly took a few shots of her while she slept. Taken together with the crazy letter, my team and I naturally thought that Mr. Wieland was a peeping Tom and had committed suicide out of a morbid infatuation for his student."

"I did think that night that I'd heard my stepfather in my room," Juno said. "So I was subconsciously quite correct on that score. Even though I was already half asleep."

"Unfortunately, we all gave it too little significance,"

Esposito said. "And, to conclude my report: in the night when he attacked you in the library, he had already prepared another suicide note, which we found in his study after his arrest. This time it was supposed to be a letter from you, Juno. He forged your handwriting amazingly well, I must say. In the case of Mr. Wieland, after all, he had made sure that the handwriting did not have to look too similar to that of the tutor. It was supposedly the scrawl of a man who had lost his mind and could no longer even write properly—a spidery scribble."

"And what were the contents of this suicide note he tried to plant on Juno?" asked Victoria.

"In coming up with this letter, Dr. Leonhardt again demonstrated his cold-blooded and very cunning ingenuity," Esposito said. "After having the tutor commit suicide seemingly out of a secret love for Juno, he stayed with the same theme. The new letter said Juno had a reciprocated love for the tutor and now could not live without him. I don't remember the exact words, but that's what it boiled down to."

"And I," Victoria said in a rough voice, "also got in his way. Like Mr. Wieland and Dr. Bachmann before me. I was probably a thorn in Sendrik's side in his plan to drive Diana mad. And besides that, I'd suggested a new specialist to examine Juno."

"According to Dr. Leonhardt's testimony—and he's adamant on this point—he didn't want to kill you, he merely wanted to intimidate you, or rather drive you out of the house," Esposito objected. "True, he would have taken your death in stride if you had broken your neck on the stairs as he pushed you down. But he wasn't explicitly aiming for that."

Again he dabbed at his forehead with his handkerchief. Either he was suffering as much as I was from the summer heat, which was setting new temperature records for us today, or this murder case was probably one of the worst he had experienced in his entire career.

Presumably both, I told myself.

"Do you see how Dr. Leonhardt varied the scheme again in the attack on you?" he said to Victoria. "With Dr. Bachmann, we were supposed to think the doctor had left in a hurry. Chris Wieland then apparently committed suicide. You, Dr. Adler, would have suffered an accident on the stairs, and Juno would have committed suicide in turn, like her secret lover the tutor."

"And I would have ended up in the loony bin," Diana added, with cold anger in her voice. "The perfect crime spree. And all for the sake of the money!"

"Many men are just after the money," Barbara chimed in. She had remained silent until now, stunned by all the heinous things that had happened in the castle of her ultra-prestigious and long-established family.

Now, however, she gave Daniel Kirsch one of her blatantly hostile looks. Surely she still thought he was a fortune hunter who only wanted to marry Juno for her money.

Esposito continued, unperturbed: "When you survived, Dr. Adler, that was also no problem for our killer; he had pushed you from behind, so it would not be possible for you to recognize him and thus expose him afterwards. So, while you were unconscious, he took you to the wine cellar to indicate that you were now also addicted to alcohol, and thereby discredit you. After that he was quite satisfied that you had moved to the hospital. He wanted to use your absence to finally put an end to his stepdaughter's life."

Esposito looked over at Pearl and me. "And your pets, Dr. Adler, were ultimately the ones who brought down the killer. If it hadn't been for these two...." He shook his head and wrinkled his forehead.

"What I really wonder about, though," he added, "is why did Pearl trash the library like that? To attract attention with the noise? Or was the poor little thing just beside herself with fear when she saw Dr. Leonhardt administering something to his stepdaughter that made her lose consciousness?"

"*The poor little thing*?" Pearl hissed. "He can't be serious!"

She got up on her paws and arched her back threateningly. That is, *she* must have thought her posturing to be threatening. I had to make a damn hard effort to look serious and not let any of my amusement show.

Esposito said, "Such a cute kitty, isn't she!" and with that, tonight's very special session of the Wednesday Evening Club came to a close.

I cheered Pearl up by suggesting a visit to the

kitchen, where Francesco spoiled us good and proper with a whole menu of delicacies. He also considered us to be the heroes of the hour and he served us a corresponding royal repast.

37

We stayed with Diana and Juno for a few more weeks. Victoria was not yet able to drive anyway, and she wanted to stand by the two of them so that they could process the terrible events and recover as well as possible. And Tim was still busy for a while in Vienna with his entrepreneurship course.

Juno's health improved slowly but steadily. Victoria made sure that her colleagues, the psychiatrist and the chief physician whom she had already suggested to Sendrik, came to the castle and took care of Juno and Diana. Even the alcohol withdrawal, which Diana began immediately, worked out quite well.

As for Daniel's marriage plans, Juno told him that she wanted to wait a little longer for the wedding ... and he did finally come to terms with it. It didn't seem to affect his love for Juno. Were his feelings real in the end, even if the two made a rather unusual couple?

Bastian promised to look for an apartment of his own, and as for Barbara, it seemed to me that Juno and Diana would be better able to defend themselves against her strict regimen from now on. And maybe she, the castle dragon, might even become a little gentler herself?

Pearl and I went to the library several more times, looking for the ghost girl, but she did not show herself to us again.

We thanked her anyway, assuming that she would hear us even if she didn't want to appear in front of us anymore. Presumably she had now retreated forever into the world of books, which she loved so much, and was fed up with both the two-leggeds and with us.

When we left the castle at the end, we still didn't know her name. Nevertheless we would probably remember her for the rest of our lives.

More from Athos and Pearl:

THE CURSE OF THE CAT GODDESS
A Case for the Master Sleuths, Book 4

In the villa of a passionate collector of Egyptian antiquities, strange incidents begin to occur around a mysterious statue of the cat goddess Bastet. Finally there is a tragic accident, and the owner of the house loses his life in a bizarre turn of events.

Luckily, Athos and Pearl are guests at the villa, together with their two humans, and they start to investigate ... but this case may prove to be the most difficult yet for the furry detective duo.

More from Alex Wagner:

If you enjoy snooping around with Athos and Pearl, why not try my other mystery series, too?

Penny Küfer Investigates—cozy crime novels full of old world charm.
Penny only has two legs, but she's a feisty and clever young detective. 😊

Murder in Antiquity—a historical mystery series from the Roman Empire.
Join shady Germanic merchant Thanar and his clever slave Layla in their backwater frontier town, and on their travels to see the greatest sights of the ancient world. Meet legionaries, gladiators, barbarians, druids and Christians—and the most ruthless killers in the Empire!

About the author

Alex Wagner lives with her husband and 'partner in crime' near Vienna, Austria. From her writing chair she has a view of an old ruined castle, which helps her to dream up the most devious murder plots.

Alex writes murder mysteries set in the most beautiful locations in Europe, and in popular holiday spots. If you love to read Agatha Christie and other authors from the Golden Age of mystery fiction, you will enjoy her stories.

www.alexwagner.at
www.facebook.com/AlexWagnerMysteryWriter
www.instagram.com/alexwagner_author

Copyright © 2022 Alexandra Wagner
Publisher: Alexandra Wagner

All rights reserved. This book or any portion
thereof may not be reproduced or used in any manner whatsoever without the express written permis-
sion of the publisher, except for the use of brief quo-
tations in a book review.
The characters in this book are entirely fictional.
Any resemblance to actual persons living or dead is
entirely coincidental.

Cover design: Estella Vukovic
Editor: Tarryn Thomas

www.alexwagner.at

Printed in Great Britain
by Amazon

17106812R00146